DEMIGODS ACADEMY

THE THREADS OF LIFE

BOOK 4

DEMIGODS ACADEMY

THE THREADS OF LIFE

ELISA S. AMORE

KIERA LEGEND

MELANY

Thick, sharp looking, green-stained stalagmites hung from the ceiling of the cave, dripping water onto the stone floor near my black combat boots. The plip-plop of the drops echoed off the walls and ground, which sparkled with green quartz. Beyond them, was a dark pool of cold ocean water; the entrance to a portal between worlds— between the demigods' academy and the regular mortal realm.

The magical passage would take us to the bay of Cala, and from there we could fly to Pecunia, to the opening ceremony of the mall that had been demolished during the Battle of the Gods.

That was what the mortals were calling it now—The Battle of the Gods.

I supposed that was what it became for them and for the world that watched through the news and social media.

For me, it was the day I lost a huge chunk of my heart and soul.

Lucian—beautiful Lucian with his golden waves, golden skin, and brilliant blue eyes that sent sparks down my body—stepped up next to me at the rocky edge of the pool, grasping my hand in his. His touch was always welcomed. "You doing okay, Blue?"

I nodded. "Yup."

Except I wasn't, and I hated that everyone asked me that question every day over the past few months since the battle. It made me want to scream, and then hit something, but I refrained. I knew that Lucian, as well as my friends, were just concerned about me since I wasn't exactly acting normal. Well, as normal as a newly minted demigod could be. Normalcy flew out the window exactly thirteen months and eight days ago, when Callie Demos—of the powerful wealthy Demos family that I lived with since I was thirteen—threw away the shadowbox she'd been given for her eighteenth birthday, and I had picked it up instead.

"Mayor Remis will be happy to see you at the ceremony," Lucian assured. "He always asks about you when I go to the mortal realm to check on things. *"How's that blue-haired, dark angel doing?"* That's what he calls you."

"Lucky me."

I guessed that a lot of people thought of me in that way. Emphasis on the *dark*. Lucian was the one who had the angel thing going on for him. When he had his huge white wings out and he was in the air, he was breathtaking.

Our friends, Jasmine, Mia, Georgina, and Ren, all stood at the edge of the pool next to us. We'd all been invited to the opening ceremony. We were the representatives of the academy now. Which was crazy to me, considering we were all recruits just over a year ago, each of us summoned by an invitation handwritten on an ancient scroll.

One of Jasmine's sly smiles made her brown eyes shine with mischief. "You ready to go swimming?"

"No, not really."

I hated using the water portal. The first time I ever used it—answering the summons to join the Gods' Army—I nearly drowned. Lucian, in fact, had been the one to save me. He dragged me out of the pool and onto the rocks right before I swallowed a bunch of water and died. That was how, and when, I got my nickname, Blue. It was the color my face turned. Although, most people thought it was because I had blue hair.

Grabbing Jasmine's hand, Mia dove with her into the water—they'd recently came out as a couple. Ren followed them, then Georgina jumped in as well. Lucian and I went in after her. Georgina's condition concerned me a bit, and I wanted to make sure she got to the portal.

She'd lost her left arm during the battle, burnt to a crisp by a fire ball from the giant, monstrous creature, Typhon. Although she was beyond resilient, and as strong as the rocks she loved, I still worried that she was going to struggle in the water. After swimming for about five minutes behind her, I realized my worries were pointless. Georgina's body moved like a dolphin's, torpedoing into the glowing blueish-white cylinder of the mystical passage.

When I first saw the portal a year ago, I thought it looked like a shining blue worm coiling through the ocean. It still looked like that as I breached its shimmering wall and was swept up into the swirling tube. I supposed it was like barreling down one of those slides at a water park, but I didn't find it as fun as the others did. Both Lucian and Ren were doing somersaults in the current as we were shot through the portal at an impossible speed.

The trip was, thankfully, no more than five minutes—I could hold my breath for longer because of my water power, but I knew the others weren't as lucky.

We were spit out into the bay, on the coast of the small city of Cala. Swimming to dock number nine, we pulled ourselves out of the sea. Once we were all out, I dried my clothes and hair using my fire ability, then helped the others with a single touch. Jasmine pouted the entire time. Despite her arguing to the contrary, I knew she was still upset that I'd taken her fire ability from her during the Battle of the Gods.

I'd actually taken power from each of my friends in order to fight against Zeus, and had yet to find a way to give it back.

Chiron, who was a great healer, and I worked on it at the academy almost every day, trying different methods, even potions, but so far, our attempts had only managed to cause me more pain than I already experienced daily. Having all five elements, water, fire, earth, lightning, and shadow swirling around inside me 24/7 wasn't pleasant. It was like being a turbulent volcano on the cusp of a massive eruption.

Once we were all dry, I watched as one by one, each of my friends unfurled a set of large white feathery wings and took to the sky like gorgeous birds of prey. Hovering in the air, they all waited for me to join them so we could fly as a flock to Pecunia. With a single thought, my shiny black wings emerged from my back—it no longer hurt when they came out—and expanded behind me. Flapping once, they lifted me into the air, and I realized, not for the first time, how much I stuck out like a sore thumb among my peers.

I was the raven to their doves.

Lucian's smile beamed at me as I hovered beside him. No matter what happened or what I'd done, he never looked at me like I was different, like there was something wrong with me. Although there most decidedly was something wrong with me, and they all knew it. I loved him for it. I didn't deserve him. He was the most noble out of us all, which was why he'd slipped so easily into a leadership role at the academy. He worked directly under Prometheus, who was one of the original founders of the academy thousands of years ago.

It took us only ten minutes to fly the ninety miles to Pecunia. As we flew over the newly built strip mall, I saw a big crowd gathered in front of a makeshift stage. Several heads tilted up as we all swooped in and slowly lowered to the ground. The sound of applause replaced the flapping of our wings as we landed, cheers erupting from the crowd with true elation.

With a huge smile splitting his round face, Mayor Remis approached us, a hand held out to greet us. He shook Lucian's hand first, then the others', but when my turn came his hold trembled a little in mine. "Welcome my friends," the mayor offered, leading us onto the stage.

As we followed, a young girl—likely no older than ten—shrunk into her mother's side when she saw me. That didn't surprise me, as for some, I was a gruesome sight.

Some days I found it hard to look in the mirror. The combination of dark tribal tattoos, piercings, and the spiderweb of scars that covered half my face and body wasn't always a pleasant sight. For me, the tattoos were a reminder of who I was before, and the scars of who I was now.

Once we were all lined up on the stage, the mayor stepped up to the microphone. "Welcome, everyone, to the grand opening of the Pecunia Victory Mall!"

The joy from the crowd became almost palpable, as more cheers and applause exploded around us.

"I'm so proud of the work we have all done to pick up the pieces from the terrible battle that happened on this land, and our coming together in fellowship to celebrate the reopening of a vital part of our community."

He paused while people clapped, and Lucian and the others made a point of joining them.

"We are honored today to have some special guests with us, who have literally flown in from the academy to celebrate this historic moment." The mayor swept his arm toward us, causing a thunderous wave of cheers. "Please help me thank the heroes of the Battle of the Gods. Lucian Perro. Jasmine Walker. Mia White. Ren Nakamura. Georgina Stewart." Pausing once more, he glanced at me. "And Melany Richmond, who was instrumental in the victory achieved here."

As everyone celebrated, I looked down at that little girl. She still had her face pressed into the side of her mother's leg. She hadn't dared risk a peek at me. I wanted to tell her that she was right to look away.

I wasn't a hero. I most definitely didn't feel like one. I felt lost and hollow. Empty.

My gaze swept the crowd, and their happy, grateful faces, and I wanted to smash every single one of them. They had no idea what had truly happened here on this battlefield. The people we lost in the fight. The ones who sacrificed everything so we could be victorious.

Nightmares about the battle still haunted me.

Jasmine had even caught me sleepwalking through the halls, and I'd nearly broken her nose with a swing of my arm when she approached me. Luckily, she was as skilled in combat as I was, and took me down before I could hurt her. I remember waking as she pressed her knee into my throat.

Movement near one of the oak trees, along the promenade that circled the new mall, suddenly drew my attention. The shadows over the ground shimmered then seemed to undulate in a familiar pattern. Without hesitation, I jumped down from the stage and walked toward the trees.

"Mel?!" Lucian called after me. "Mel, where are you going?"

I didn't stop. I couldn't.

When I got to the trees, I reached out to touch the shadows, hoping my hand would dissolve into them, and I could travel to the place I truly wanted to be. Although, without its master, I wasn't sure it still existed.

"Hades?" I whispered.

Instead of disappearing into the shade, my hand hit the grass and my fist tore the green blades. Disappointment flooded me and I felt like throwing up. Still something was blocking me from moving through the shadows to the underworld. Something, or *someone*. I longed to visit the dark and hollow halls of Hades' palace. I wanted to see my friends there. The Furies and Cerberus. I even missed Charon—despite of how he used to creep around, his skeletal face devoid of any emotion. With Hades gone, could they not leave the underground dwelling?

Standing, I smacked my fist into the trunk of the giant oak in frustration. Pieces of bark and wood crumbled off the tree from the blow. Any more force and I would've knocked the tree over, roots and all. The few people nearby noticeably moved away.

Movement came from behind me, and I turned around, expecting to see Lucian or Georgina coming to check on me—as they always did when I acted out.

"Melany? I can't believe it's you…"

Instead, I came face to face with Callie Demos, the girl I grew up with, and the one I took the shadowbox from so I could escape to the academy. The last time I saw her was at her eighteenth birthday party, when I was just some rebellious loner and my adoptive mother, Sophia, was still alive.

CHAPTER TWO

MELANY

"Hey, Callie."

She hadn't changed much. Still possessed long golden blond hair and perfect features. She'd always reminded me of Aphrodite with her beauty and grace, but after dealing with the Goddess herself, I amended my comparison. Although Callie had been a selfish, spoiled brat in the past, she was nowhere near the narcissistic, sociopathic level where Aphrodite operated.

Callie's gaze swept over me as she shook her head. She reached for my hand, but quickly changed her mind—probably remembering we were never the touchy feely type of friends, despite growing up together in the same house. "I can't believe you're here. We didn't know what to think when you just disappeared like that. Never in my wildest dreams did I ever think you would turn out to be some demigod hero."

I shrugged. "Me either."

"How did you even get into the academy? You never received a shadowbox, did you?"

"No, but something happened when I took yours."

Her brow furrowed between her bright blue eyes, letting me know how pissed off she was. I'd seen that look more often than not. "Did you take my spot or something?"

"It doesn't work like that. Believe me. At first, that was what I thought happened, but I learned later—from Hephaistos, who makes the boxes—that only the chosen person can actually breach the portal and get there."

The way she looked at me, I didn't think she quite believed me. I had a feeling it wouldn't really matter what I told her. She would always think I stole her chance to be one of us, that I stole her chance at glory. I could've told her that there was no such thing. Being at the academy had only brought me pain and suffering. There was no glory in what I'd been through.

Before I could say anything more, Callie's mother,

Mrs. Demos, came up beside her. I thought she might smile at me, but the look on her face was one of sympathy. She did reach for my hand though. "Melany, I'm so happy to see you. When we saw you on that stage, we couldn't believe it."

"I'm happy to see you too."

Her gaze lingered over my scars. "What happened to you? You look like you've been…"

"The price of being a demigod, I suppose."

Unease marred her features, and she swallowed. "You were always very brave."

That surprised me. I never believed Mrs. Demos thought much about me. She'd certainly always been kind—as kind as a person could be to the daughter of the head housekeeper in their estate—but I never knew she held any kind of opinion about me one way or another.

"Thank you." I gave her a small smile, then looked behind her, scanning the crowd milling about us. "Is Mr. Demos here?"

Her face paled, as did Callie's, and she set a hand on her daughter's arm. "He died in the earthquake. The same one where Sophia…"

When her words faltered, I nodded and swallowed, not wanting to talk about my adoptive mother. "I'm sorry. Mr. Demos was always kind to me."

Mrs. Demos grabbed my hand again. "And Sophia was an amazing woman. We feel her loss as well."

Uncomfortable, I looked past them to Lucian and Georgina, who were walking toward us. "I need to go." I pulled my hand out from hers. "It was good to see you."

"You too," Mrs. Demos offered.

Before I could walk away, Callie pulled me to her and hugged me close. "Stay safe. Don't die, okay?"

Unable to ignore the irony, I gave her a tight smile. "I already have."

Lucian cupped my cheek when I joined the others, and I leaned into him. I sensed watchful gazes on me, and I imagined Callie was watching our exchange—Lucian was the kind of guy she would go gaga for easily. She was probably wondering how a guy like him could ever like a girl like me. Sometimes I still wondered that too. He was way too good for me, and always had been.

"Everything good?"

"That was Callie Demos and her mom."

He looked toward them, then nodded. I'd told Lucian everything about my life before the academy. "How was that reunion?"

I shrugged. "Fine. They're from a past that doesn't matter anymore." My wings unfurled behind me, and I flapped them as Lucian frowned at me. "Are we ready to head back?"

"If nobody minds, I want to fly over to New Haven and check in on my family," Jasmine asked as she grabbed Mia's hand in hers. "Do you want to come with?"

Mia blushed and I could see the twinkle in her green eyes. "Really?"

Jasmine shrugged. "Why not?"

"Do you think your parents will like me?"

"Of course they will." Pulling Mia closer, Jasmine kissed her, which just made Mia blush even more.

Lucian nodded. "Have fun. Just remember to be back before nightfall. Prometheus is a lot more lenient than Zeus was, but there are still rules."

Jasmine's white wings flapped swiftly and took her into the air—they were so majestic against her dark skin. Mia followed, and they flew high into the sky, disappearing over the tops of the big oak trees.

"Anyone else need a side trip?" Lucian asked.

Both Georgina and Ren shook their heads, yet I knew why Ren didn't speak. I'd snuck him out of the academy a few weeks ago, and took him through one of the shadow gates to his home in Japan. Unfortunately, it hadn't gone as smoothly as I'd hoped, we'd ended up in Iceland the first time, but eventually made it to his home. I wasn't supposed to be using the shadows to travel anymore, everyone, especially Lucian for obvious reasons, thought it was bad for my psyche, but I did almost every night anyway, looking for a way back to the underworld hall. Lucian and my friends thought I was looking for a way back to *him*, but I knew he was dead. Probably languishing away in Elysium with his first love, Persephone.

"Are you sure, Gina?" I asked, concerned. As far as I knew, she hadn't seen her family since she arrived at the academy over a year ago. "Kios isn't that far. Maybe a half hour flight."

She shook her head again, her gaze on the ground. "I'm good." Flapping her wings, she lifted into the sky. "Let's get going before we lose the light. I still have some gardening to do in the greenhouse. Dionysus needs some new herbs for his potions."

"His alcoholic beverages, you mean." Ren chuckled, then took to the air.

I didn't press her on her decision. She must've had her reasons, and I suspected they had mostly to do with the loss of her arm and her earth power. I wanted to tell her that I was doing everything I could to find a way to give her ability back to her, but I also didn't want to get her hopes up. She was definitely depressed.

Most days, she spent her time outside in the

gardens, digging in the dirt. One time, I found her liter-ally sitting in a giant hole she dug in the ground. I worried that she was contemplating never coming out of it, but I hauled her out of there, and we went to the dining hall to gorge on ice cream and cake while Dionysus entertained us with his new DJ set. The party God loved his dubstep.

We flew to Cala, landing on the main dock in the pier. There were a few mortals around, tending to their boats, and they stopped to watch us land. Their smiles and waves greeted us, now that they were used to us demigods flying in and out of the mortal realm.

Before the big battle, our existence had been very secretive. Not anymore.

We were all out of the closet, so to speak.

As we made our way to dock nine, so we could dive into the water and swim to the portal, shouts from nearby drew my attention. I looked down a few docks to see a woman crouched by a man slumped on the wood, clutching at him and screaming.

Immediately, Lucian and I launched into the air and flew over to them. The man laying on the dock clutched at his chest; his eyes rolled back into his head.

"Howard! Oh Gods, Howard!" The woman shrieked, tears running down her cheeks.

Lucian nodded to the other man standing in shock

near the boat. "Call for an ambulance." He approached the couple, crouching next to the man. "Looks like he's having a heart attack." Lucian gently removed the woman's hands from her husband's shirt, then unbuttoned it and pulled the two parts away so he was bare-chested. When Lucian went to press his hands to the man's chest, he paused, remembering he didn't possess his lightning power anymore, and looked up at me. "Mel, you'll need to shock him."

"You're just kids! You don't know what you're doing!" the woman shrieked as I knelt by the guy, rubbing my hands together. Sparks sizzled around my fingers.

She wasn't entirely wrong. We were just kids, young adults to be exact, and I sure didn't know what the hell I was doing. Lucian had more faith in me than was probably wise.

"Ma'am, Melany here has brought people back from death. She brought me back, so she can help Howard."

Lucian had a gift with people. Everyone liked him. Trusted him. He was a born leader. It helped that he looked like a golden God sent here from Olympus. The woman nodded, and grew calm, as she watched me set my hands on her husband's chest.

His heart had stopped. I couldn't feel any beats of it

under my palms. Closing my eyes, I gathered every tendril of electricity inside me and pushed it out through my hands. Howard jolted off the dock, then landed back with a thump. Still, no heartbeat. So, I hit him again with a small bolt of lightning. The body jerked off the ground again.

Shadows slowly drew across the wooden floor, shrouding me and Howard in darkness. I'd seen this before when Lucian had died in my arms. Surveying the gloom, I saw a form taking shape as it slowly moved toward me. My heart raced as hope sprung in my chest. Although I knew it wasn't Hades approaching—Gods, how I wanted it to be—the sight of death was still startling.

Draped in a black cloak and carrying a long, heavy-looking silver scythe, the tall figure loomed over me. I stood and faced him. "Hello, Thanatos."

"Melany." His voice was a harsh and raspy buzzing in my ears.

"Have you come to claim Howard?"

Thanatos looked down at the mortal laying prone at my feet, and shook his hooded head. He didn't possess a face, so it was hard to tell what he was think-ing. "I have no thread for this man."

My brows creased in confusion. "What does that mean?"

"It means this mortal won't die, even though it is his time."

Glancing down at Howard, I found that his eyes were opening. The shadows dissipated around me until I was no longer alone in the darkness. Lucian was there again, smiling. The woman was laughing, and in the midst of tears, thanking me.

"You saved him!" She grabbed me and pulled me into a tight hug. Her scent smelled of vanilla and despair. I pulled away from her, and looked back down at Howard. He was slowly trying to sit up while Lucian helped him.

Dropping to her knees, the woman hugged her husband. "Oh, my Gods, I can't believe it."

The sound of a siren grew near announcing the ambulance arrived at the pier.

Howard looked around, confusion evident on his face. "Wh-what happened?"

"You had a heart attack," his wife explained, tears still springing from her eyes.

"I did?" His gaze eventually landed on me, and his eyes nearly popped out of his head. "You! I saw you in the darkness."

"She saved your life," the woman crowed.

Howard lifted his hand toward me. "Thank you."

I was hesitant to take it, but felt like I had to with

everyone watching and judging. The moment I touched his skin, a cold, creeping sensation feathered up my arm. Frowning, I peered at him. He looked off. Odd. Not normal.

Everyone possessed an aura around them. Different types of energies swirling either in harmony or conflict along their bodies. Demigods and Gods had auras too, but they were brighter; the colors more vibrant. Apollo had taught us to see and read them, but Howard didn't have one anymore. It was like his life energy had faded, leaving an empty shell in its place.

"You're welcome." I pulled my hand away from his and rubbed my palm on my pants. That cold, creeping feeling still clung to my skin like an icy spiderweb. Unfolding my wings, I flew back to dock nine and dove into the water, but there was still no relief from the odd sensation choking me. I couldn't get away from the man fast enough.

CHAPTER THREE

MELANY

It took merely a couple of minutes to get through the portal, then I was climbing the rocky edge of the pool in the cave—careful not to scrape my knees and elbows like I'd done previously. I knew the others were right behind me, but I didn't stop and wait for them. I needed some space. I needed some time to myself. Before I could reach the exit though, I heard Lucian running to catch up with me. I sighed in frustration, hoping he hadn't heard me.

"Mel, wait up."

I stopped, because I could hear the slight panic in his voice. He always acted like he was expecting me to just vanish into thin air. Like he was hanging onto me only by the very tips of his fingers. In some ways, that was true. I had vanished before, although it hadn't been on purpose. Hades had taken me, and I'd told Lucian that, but I wasn't sure he believed it.

"Are you okay? That was pretty intense back there."

"I'm tired of being asked that." I shook my head. "I'm not okay, all right?! And if that's not obvious, then you're not looking very hard." I stormed away from him, not caring if he followed or not.

Well, actually, I didn't want him to follow me. I really didn't want to deal with him or anyone for that matter right now.

Gods, what I wouldn't give to be alone!

When I came out of the cave, I had to put my hand up to my face to block the hot rays of sun greeting me. The sky was a robin's egg blue, so pure and clear, and always a joy to see on a good day. Although, it hadn't felt like a good day in a long time, and I didn't feel much joy right now.

Seeing Callie and her mom in Pecunia had brought back a lot of memories, not all of them bad, mind you. Callie and I hadn't been best friends or anything, but we'd had a few fun days together. Yet, seeing them also made me think about Sophia, and how much I missed her and would never see her again.

The regret for how I left her that night still clung to me. Still choked me in the middle of the night, when I dreamed of her.

Sharp, gray stone spires, jutting out of the four turrets of the academy loomed in the distance as I walked along the wide cobblestone path leading up to it. I remembered when I first saw the building. I thought it looked like a great Gothic cathedral, or a castle from medieval England built to withstand any battle siege. It was all dark stone and sharp edges.

The spindly trees that lined the path still looked like decrepit old hags to me, reaching out to those who passed by it. I always wondered why they were so barren when everything else around the land grew in vivid abundance. I'd always meant to ask Demeter about that, but never got around to it.

Instead of going straight into the academy, I veered off the path and headed toward the large hedge maze. The entrance was guarded by two stone soldiers, their swords raised to fight. The rumor around the school was that all the statues were once people, turned to stone by the fierce gaze of Medusa. After having fought against her in a mock battle during training, and during the real thing against the giant Titan called Typhon, I still couldn't say if that rumor was true or not.

The gorgon was an enigma, but I would say that I

never wanted to get on her really bad side, which was ironic since I wasn't sure she had any good ones.

I entered the maze; it had become my sanctuary since coming here. It was huge, with a multitude of twisted, complicated turns and dead ends, but I'd always known how to get to the middle. At first, I thought it had just been dumb luck, or skill, but I knew now that I'd been led there by the shadows swirling inside of me. This beautiful, terrible darkness that I'd embraced and even learned to love. I ached for it now more than ever.

Reaching the center, I hoped to find that darkness waiting for me.

Instead, I found Prometheus with the first small group of new recruits for the school since the battle in Pecunia, and the regime change at the academy. With him standing at over seven feet tall, I was surprised I didn't see the top of his dark curly hair over one of the hedges. Out of all the Titans, he was definitely the most human looking, but that didn't make him any less formidable.

He perked up when he saw me step out from the corner. "Oh, we have a real treat for you today," he announced.

Fifteen heads turned toward me as one. Eyes widened, a rush of whispers escaped them.

"It's her!"

"She's the Dark Angel of Pecunia."

"Her scars are so cool!"

"I heard she went insane."

"Didn't she kill one of her own?"

Smiling, Prometheus reached out a hand toward me, his kind brown eyes crinkling at the sides. "Melany, come and speak to the new recruits."

I didn't want to talk to anyone, and I certainly didn't think I was the best person to welcome these wide-eyed, naïve kids. Lucian had been chosen to be the one to do the big speech during the first days of their training. He looked trustworthy and charming while I was told, in no uncertain terms, to remain scarce—especially at the start.

They were going to have to eventually deal with me when it came to training with the elements. I'd been chosen to replace Zeus to teach the lightning class.

For a brief moment, I considered rejecting his request, but I knew I still had duties to uphold here. Not only was I still in training, as were my peers, but I'd been given new responsibilities since liberating the academy from Zeus' lightning-fisted rule, and setting Prometheus free from Tartarus—where Zeus had imprisoned him for a few millennia. I'd been instrumental, as well as Lucian, and my friends, in reinstating

Prometheus as headmaster like he had been thousands of years prior.

Although, I didn't really consider this a way of thanking me. Instead, I should've been put on the "I don't have to do any inspirational speeches EVER" list. I hated speaking in front of a bunch of people, and I wasn't any good at it. Despite my reservations, I walked toward the group, and stood beside Prometheus. I imagined I probably looked like an insect next to him. An ugly, deformed one.

"Ah, hello, welcome to the academy." Unconsciously, I rubbed my hand over the lightning scars along my right arm, feeling a little bit vulnerable as fifteen pairs of eyes gaped at me. It was like being at a zoo, but I was the one in the cage.

"As I'm sure you are all aware, Melany was the one who discovered the Titans were being used by certain Gods to do their bidding. She led the charge into battle against Zeus, Aphrodite, and Ares."

Swirling murmurs flew into the air like buzzing bees with his statement.

"She's a hero," said one perky looking guy with ginger hair and honey-colored eyes.

Prometheus' hand rested on my shoulder, completely encompassing it. "She is a hero. And I hope that you will all learn from her, and the others at the academy, about what that truly means. It's not about fame and glory, but sacrifice for the greater good, for your fellow human being."

As I stood there, a sudden rush of cold surged over me. It felt like icy fingers crawled up my spine. It wasn't something I'd felt before. Not like the cool tingling brush of shadows as they crept over my skin, but something else entirely… and it was coming from the group of recruits.

Searching for the source of this feeling of malice and ominous dread, I met each of their gazes, but couldn't lock on the point of origin. Everyone just looked like what they were supposed to—eager eighteen-year-old recruits—and nothing else. Maybe one of them was Aphrodite in disguise, coming for her revenge on me. She was an expert shapeshifter, but I was certain that she was still locked away with her lover, Ares, the God of War, in the barren hellscape of Tartarus.

A hand went up in the crowd; it belonged to a sleek looking brunette. She had a similar look to what Callie had—primped, poised, and privileged. "Can you tell us about how you beat Zeus? I mean, he's the most powerful God of them all, and you are…" she waved a hand at me, "like, just a girl."

I had an urge to fling some fire or lightning her way,

to prove to her that I wasn't "just a girl", but we were interrupted by the flapping sound of large wings. Everyone looked up as Lucian soared overhead, gently landing near the white wood, and stone gazebo. The dark sensation aimed toward me suddenly vanished.

All the girls in the group tittered at the sight of him; one boy did as well. I didn't blame them; Lucian was a beautiful sight to behold. All gold and white, sparkling like the sun and everything good and pure in the world, I thought he could definitely give Apollo a run for his money. He most definitely did in my eyes.

"We are truly blessed with visitors today," Prometheus offered, waving toward Lucian. "Come, Lucian, and say hello to our new recruits."

Smiling, Lucian approached the group as he folded his angelic wings against his back. "Hello."

That sent more giggles through the impressionable group. The two girls standing at the front looked like they were going to either pee their pants or pass out.

I supposed if I was a jealous person, I would've grabbed Lucian and pulled him in for a long, wet, hot kiss, to prove to everyone that he belonged to me. But I wasn't the jealous girlfriend type. Still, I couldn't help growling at the two girls. Startled, they both took a few steps backward. I smirked in triumph. Sometimes it was the little things that brought me pleasure.

Prometheus' look of praise transferred to Lucian, where, I was sure everyone would agree, it belonged. "You've just returned from Pecunia, I'm told, where there was a great celebration for the opening of the new community mall."

"Yes." Lucian glanced at me briefly, then to the group. "We were there with the mayor. It was a great ceremony; an important one."

"Are you going to be teaching us, Lucian?" asked the same brunette who had questioned me.

He nodded. "I will be, yes, alongside Heracles."

That incited more excited whispers and giggles from his "fans". It was becoming annoying, and I just about took to the air, to fly away from it.

"It's time for us to move on with the tour," Prometheus politely interjected, and I wondered if he could sense my growing impatience. He gestured to the path in the maze that would lead them out to the back of the academy, and the new training field. "Thank you, Melany and Lucian."

"You're welcome," Lucian assured.

I just nodded as he led the students away from the gazebo and back into the hedges.

When they were gone, I rubbed my arms again. Although the source of the malice had moved on with the group, the remnants of it still lingered on my body.

A shiver ran down my spine, and I couldn't get rid of it. It felt like I'd never get warm again. The sensation was so deep. I'd never felt such cold dread before, not from the Furies, not from Medusa, not even from Hades, the Lord of Darkness himself.

It was an entirely new level of horror, one I wasn't sure I wanted to unearth.

CHAPTER FOUR

LUCIAN

*W*hen the group had disappeared behind the hedge, I turned toward Melany. She looked drawn, even a bit spooked. Like something had startled her. It must've been serious to unsettle her, as she was usually the one to do the unsettling.

I considered asking her if she was okay, but she'd already shouted at me for that, so I refrained. It was difficult to not want to wrap her in my arms to keep her safe and secure, but I knew she wouldn't thank me for it.

She'd probably bite my head off.

Melany had always been surly, ever since I met her,

but since the battle and the aftermath, she'd reached a new level of impatience and sullenness. I wasn't the only one to notice. Both Jasmine and Georgina had come to me with concerns about Melany's mental well being. Unfortunately, they too, didn't know what to do or how to help her.

And I hated that it most likely had everything to do with losing Hades.

"I'd forgotten that the new recruits would be here today," I offered, trying to call her eyes to me. "With all that's happened, it's hard to keep up with events. But like everything else, life has to go on."

Melany didn't answer, she just wrapped her arms around herself and shivered. I frowned. It wasn't cold. Quite the opposite in fact. I found it to be a pleasantly warm day. Most days at the academy were nice and sunny. We weren't affected by most weather here, being in a separate realm of existence had its advantages. Although, I did miss snow. I'd been an expert snowboarder in the past.

Before I could ask about her reaction and have her yell at me again, she finally focused on me. "I felt something dark from that group of recruits."

"Dark, how? Maybe you were sensing someone who has an affinity to the shadows, like you."

"No, it felt different. It was like a sensation of terror

and fear. As if something catastrophic was about to happen."

The way she spoke concerned me. As long as I'd known Melany, she'd never been afraid of anything. Not the training, not the trials, not even the Gods. Yet, there was fear in her voice. If she was frightened, it was definitely troubling.

"Are you sure it came from the new recruits?"

Narrowing her eyes, her gaze darkened as she looked at me. "What does that mean?"

I sighed. I hated that just about everything I said to her lately, she took in the wrong way. She was constantly irritated, and I suspected I was mostly the source of that irritation. It had been days, maybe even more than a week, since we spent alone time together. Just the two of us, in each other's arms. I couldn't remember the last time she'd kissed me with any passion. It was usually just a quick peck on the lips and a pat on the back.

"It means that you've been out of sorts lately. You're not yourself."

"So, I'm making this up?"

"I didn't say that. But maybe you're manifesting it from within. You've been depressed."

She glared at me.

I reached for her, but she pulled away from my hand.

"You have every reason to feel that way, Mel. You've lost… important people in your life. But we all have. Everyone has suffered, and we need to move on. We need to take that pain and turn it into something positive, something we can use to continue our training, so we can protect others."

"This is more than that. It's not about Hades," she said with a sharp edge in her voice.

"I didn't say it was about him, but when you don't let me touch you, I have to wonder." The second it was out of my mouth I knew I made a huge mistake.

"I can't believe you're making this about your dick." She sneered, and the lightning scars along her face, neck, chest, and arm started to glow. It was faint, a soft, white luminance, but it was growing with every deep inhale of air she took.

"C'mon. That's not fair, Mel. You know it's not."

She turned away from me, but I didn't let her ignore this conversation. It was inevitable. I knew it, and she knew it. We'd been dancing around it for months. Maybe even longer than since the battle. Maybe this talk had to happen ever since she disappeared into the shadows, and spent almost a year in the underworld with Hades.

He had not only been at her side, training her in the dark arts, but he'd also been seducing her mind, body, and soul. Then he sacrificed himself to save her. I wondered if that had been the final move of his plan, to secure his complete and utter dominance over her. His possession of her.

How could I ever hope to compete with a dead man?

She walked toward the gazebo, probably a subconscious instinct to be near him, but I stayed right on her heels. It was here that Hades first showed himself to her, strumming a guitar, and singing. Intriguing her. Seducing her.

"I won't let you walk away from this anymore. From us."

Melany whipped around. "What do you want from me?"

"I want to have a rational conversation about us."

Shaking her head, she sighed, mumbling under breath. "You're so gods-damned needy."

"What? What did you say?"

"I said you're so needy. You're like a child sometimes. Always looking for validation from others, from the professors, from our peers, from me. It's tiring."

"Wow. Tell me how you really feel, Mel." I smirked.

"I'm sorry, Lucian. You wanted to have this conversation. So, we're having it."

"I didn't realize I was such a burden on you."

When her gaze met mine it was direct and harsh, and I wanted to look away. "I can't hold you together. Not when I can barely hold myself together. I can't be what you want me to be, because I have no idea who I am anymore. I'm broken, Lucian. And you can't fix me. I don't want you to."

With emotions spilling over, I swallowed and reached to touch her face. She didn't let me. I dropped my hand to my side feeling my heart starting to split apart. "If you need more time, you can have it, Mel. You can have as much as you need. I won't pressure you."

She just kept looking at me. I suspected if Melany had been a regular girl, there would've been tears in her eyes, but she wasn't regular. There were no tears. At least not for me, anyway.

"But you are pressuring me. With every look you give me."

I couldn't stand here next to her and not touch her. I could feel the sorrow emanating off of her. It was killing me to know that I couldn't help her. That she wouldn't even let me try to console her.

Risking a step closer, I reached for her again. My

hand finally cupped her cheek, and I slowly pulled her close until she was in my arms. Her body was warm against mine, getting warmer. The glow from her scars intensified. Power, chaotic and fierce, swirled around inside her. I could see it swimming in the depths of her blue eyes, could feel it oozing from every pore of her skin.

"I love you, Blue. Together we can figure it out. I know we can. Don't give up on us."

I leaned down and brushed my lips against hers. She let me do it, didn't pull away, but she didn't reciprocate. It was like kissing a mannequin. When I pulled back, her eyes also started to glow. Her skin became so hot, I had to let her go or else get burned.

Melany was like a white star on the precipice of exploding.

"I don't love you," she declared, her voice robotic, unfeeling.

It was so very unlike her, but I wondered if I was just lying to myself to stop the pain blossoming in my chest. She had fundamentally changed. She was different. Not just because she had extreme amounts of power swirling inside her. Power I knew she didn't ask for. Power I knew that caused her pain.

"I don't believe you. You're just trying to push me away. Again."

She shrugged. "Tell yourself that if it makes it easier. I don't care either way. I'm done worrying about everyone else."

Her words hurt. I didn't want them to, but they did, gutting me to the bone. Had I been blind to her indifference toward me? It was possible, with everything else that had been happening. I'd been busy helping Prometheus and the other Gods with the changes in the academy. I had been helping Athena with the new learning center that had been her well-guarded ancient library. Even preparing with Heracles to be his assistant in hand-to-hand combat training for the new recruits, and the continued training for my peers.

Melany had been busy too with working alongside Hephaistos, constructing the tribute statues for the hall of heroes, and working with Chiron on trying to find a way to give back the powers she'd taken to defeat Zeus. I knew that had been tiring for her, as it wasn't an easy process. Certainly, couples went through things like this, didn't they?

Well, maybe not exactly this, as we were demigods in an academy run by Gods, so our circumstances were definitely unique. It didn't mean we were falling out of love with each other. It couldn't be that.

"We need some time together. Just the two of us." I

unfurled my wings and flapped them. "Let's go flying, like we used to. Go to our spot by the lake."

"It's not that, Lucian. I wish it were."

Grabbing her hand, I winced at how hot it was, but I wasn't ready to let her go, no matter how hard she pushed me away. "I love you, Blue. That's never going to change. You need time and space, then take it. I'll be here when you want to come back."

As her lightning scars flared, I was forced to lift my other hand to shield my eyes from the glare. The sudden white flash produced spots in my vision, and I tried to blink them away. Her hand in mine grew too hot to hold, and I dropped it, taking a step away from her. The last time I'd seen her body react like that, she was in the middle of the battle with Zeus, when anger, fury, and pain congealed together and lashed out of her.

"Blue? Are you okay? Can I take you to Chiron?"

"Stop asking me that!!"

Snapping from her back abruptly, her wings shot her into the air like a lightning bolt. Melany zipped across the sky and disappeared over the tallest tower of the academy. I considered going after her, but I didn't think she'd appreciate it. With the way she was acting, she might even try to hurt me. It was clear she wasn't in control of herself right now. Definitely not of her emotions. Those were what had triggered the power surge in her body, I was sure of it. That was how she had managed to defeat Zeus. With all the rage, fear, and love that roared like a savage beast inside of her.

With a flap of my wings I rose into the air as well. I wasn't going to follow her. I was going to find everyone that loved her, and together, maybe we could figure out how to help her. I'd go to Chiron first, then Hephaistos and Demeter, then to Jasmine, Georgina, and Ren.

There had to be a way, because I feared that if she kept on this ravaged path, she wasn't going to make it. Melany was the strongest person I knew, but even the fiercest beings had limits.

Even the brightest white star in the sky could run out of power, and fade into the dark.

CHAPTER FIVE

MELANY

I wasn't completely sure where I was flying to when I shot up into the air, all I knew was I had to get away before I did something awful that I couldn't take back. I knew I'd hurt Lucian anyway. Words had power and I had wielded them like a sword, cutting as deep as I could.

It was necessary. He would understand that eventually.

As I soared over the spires of the academy, I caught sight of the large green lake Lucian had mentioned. A place we had visited together several times. It was where we'd had sex for the first time, and I knew where I needed to go.

Touching down on the water's edge, I took in a deep breath, reveling in the peace and quiet there. Soon, it would be active with new recruits as they learned to control the water element with Poseidon. Memories of the water trial here came to me. We had to swim across the four-mile lake, before the nine-headed hydra living within its depths captured us. Yet, as I looked across the calm surface, it seemed like a million years ago.

A new thought entered my mind, and I walked into the surrounding woods on the hunt. It didn't take me long to find what I was searching. Once, it had been a giant oak tree, tall, and thirty feet wide. The branches had been so big and heavy that a few of them touched the ground, spreading out along the forest floor, much like a giant spider with eight sprawling legs.

Now, it was merely a stump. A huge stump. Gone was the majestic giant tree I had admired. It was cut down when Aphrodite, Ares, and their minions tried to find a way to get to me in the underworld. They had failed.

Lucian told me about the tree, claiming it had been the path he, Jasmine, and Georgina had taken to try to find me when I was whisked away through the shadows, disappearing without a trace. He'd given the witch, Hecate—who'd lived in the tree—his blood for safe passage down into Hades realm.

I knocked on the stump, curious of whether she still lived inside. The last time I saw her was when she'd knocked on the doors of Hades' Hall, looking for sanctuary. She fought with us in the war, but after everything was over, I hadn't seen her again. I wasn't sure what had happened to her.

The tree didn't open, like Lucian had described, Hecate obviously wasn't at home. More likely, she had found another place to live. I was probably grasping at straws, desperate to find a way back to the underworld. Though, I wasn't exactly sure why I needed to go back.

Clearly, some of that need had everything to do with missing Hades, wanting to be around rooms and things that reminded me of him, but there was something else driving me as well. A need to retreat. To escape the pointed, pitying looks, and hushed whispers about my mental and physical state. I was tired of everyone looking at me like I was either going to break apart into a million pieces, or explode with enough shrapnel to massacre the entire academy.

I could feel the rage swirling around inside me. It was getting worse, even while Chiron was trying to help me separate the elemental abilities I carried. I supposed there was only so much power one person could handle. I wasn't a God; my body wasn't designed to hold this much energy within safely. I had to have an outlet. The force of it had to go somewhere.

My hands rested on top of the oak tree stump, and instantly, the earth power I'd taken from Georgina rose to the surface. I could feel it reaching out to the tree, to the bushes, and to the ground. It tickled the tips of my fingers as I let it out slowly. I didn't want to raze the woods with a sudden burst of energy.

At first, it flowed out of me in a trickle, then it became a flood. I couldn't rein it in as tendrils of power curled around the tree trunk, then dug into the damp earth. Deep inside, I could feel every tree in the forest, every blade of grass, rock, and granule of soil. It was too much to experience all at once. I felt like I was being buried alive.

I tried to pull away from it, both mentally and physically, but it was as if my hands were glued to the wood. Giving it everything I had, I tugged back, and the skin on my palms seemed to stretch. Eyes wide, I was surprised it didn't peel off. When the pain curled up my arms, I stopped. There had to be a way out of this. I couldn't be stuck.

Instead of pulling back again, I pushed forward. Maybe I needed to expend all the pent-up earth energy

I had inside, to be free of it. Concentrating on the tree stump in front of me, I pushed every wisp of power I could gather into it, through it.

My hands burned as the force rippled through me, and out of every pore in my palms. I watched the tree stump shake as if there was an earthquake right under my feet, until, with a loud crack, it split apart, releasing me from the hold the wood had. I stumbled backward, my arms flailing out to the sides when I nearly fell. Every muscle in my body quivered with exertion.

After I stabilized myself, I approached the stump again. Peering into the large crevice I made in the wood, I found that it went down deep into the ground.

I'd created a hole about three feet wide through the dirt and rock.

Summoning a fire ball between my hands, I dropped it into the crater. It hit the bottom quickly, so the hole wasn't too deep, but it appeared I'd dug right into an already formed tunnel by the looks of the smoothed-out sides and floor. Was that the way that Lucian had taken to the underworld to find me? I had every intention of finding out.

Without hesitation, I climbed onto what was left of the tree, and slowly lowered myself into the hole. It was a tight fit, and I had to squirm my way through it, but eventually, I was dangling from my fingers. Finally letting go, I dropped about two feet until I landed on the hard-packed earth of the tunnel.

I picked up the fireball from the ground, then started to walk through the dirt passage. After some time, although I couldn't distinguish how long, the path opened up into a huge cavern and marsh, illuminated by the moonlight that cascaded through breaks in the high, rocky ceiling. Beyond that, I could hear the rush of raging water.

Laughter burst out of me freely. I knew that sound. It was the crashing of the river, Styx. My nose lifted as I inhaled the thick stale air, and laughed again. I was so close I could literally taste it. I was almost back home.

Although I wanted to, I refrained from running across the marsh. When I reached the water's edge, my gaze found the cave that lead to the giant metal doors of Hades' Hall. I just had to cross the river. Unfurling my wings, since it was likely the best way over, I flapped them to lift me up, but it was like moving through a thick gel. I couldn't get any altitude. I managed to get off the ground a few inches, but the force of the air on my wings, brought me right back down. I wasn't going to be able to fly over there.

Crouching on the bank I submersed my fingers into the water. Maybe I could literally part the water and walk through it, but the water wasn't reacting to me. I couldn't even grasp it. It just sifted through my fingers like sand on a beach.

Frowning, I reached for the rocks along the riverbed, thinking I could build something to walk across, but again I was denied. The rocks weren't listening to me. Nothing worked down here. I couldn't get any of my elemental powers to work. What good were they?!

Frustration filled me so hard and fast that my hands began to shake. I was so close. It wasn't fair.

"Hades, help me!" The scream ripped from the ache in my chest, my voice echoing across the cave, and bouncing off the stone walls back to me.

The words pinged, almost seeming to amplify, mocking me with each syllable. I dropped to my knees on the river shore and considered diving into the black river to swim across, despite the violent current. Maybe I would make it, maybe I wouldn't. I had to try something.

Before I could plunge into the cold, murky water, the surface of it started to bubble. For a moment, I wondered if it was a residual effect from what I had done, but soon realized that something was emerging from the river.

A large black form rose from the water like a monolith, and I gasped, as the shape formed—three large triangular heads turned toward me. Three sets of glowing red eyes glared down at my face like lasers. Three mouths opened, revealing sets of razor-sharp teeth—saliva dripping from between the jowls.

Joy filled my heart as I got to my feet, and three large tongues rolled out from gaping maws, nearly bathing me in drool. "Hello boy, I missed you!"

Cerberus barked. The multiple sounds echoed like thunder that made the stone walls shake.

Laughter left me once again, and I reached for him when he bent low, letting me give a good scratching to his ears. He yipped, mewling in pleasure, and I swiftly climbed onto his back.

I didn't have to tell him where I wanted to go.

He walked across the river and pulled himself up onto the opposite shore. My fingers curled into his fur, holding on tightly as he shook the wetness off his body. I was almost thrown off, but I knew how to stay on as I had before. The giant hellhound bounded into the cave, seemingly happy to have me riding on his back like we'd done several times in the past.

The last time being the Battle of the Gods in Pecunia, which had me wondering how he faired without his master. He looked well fed and groomed, so thankfully, someone was taking care of him.

Ten minutes later we arrived at the looming metal

doors to Hades' Hall. For a moment, I thought about knocking, but I didn't know if anyone would be there. Instead, I rubbed Cerberus' head. "Can you open the doors, boy?"

Standing on his hind legs, he slapped his two huge front paws against the iron. The doors creaked open, and he leapt inside. The hall was dark. No fires flickered from the cracks in the walls and floor like they had when I'd lived here. It was more dreary than usual, which was a shame because lit up, the hall was darkly beautiful—much like the man to whom it belonged.

I slid off the hound's back and moved to one wall, producing flames along my fingertips. Lowering my hands into the crevices I waited. In seconds, the flames erupted along the floor and slits in the walls, until the hall glowed with a warm orange luminance. I took it all in, my heart swelling. It was just as I remembered it.

Movement on one side made me whip around, my hand instantly going to the dagger strapped to my waist. A dark shape flitted out from the shadows, its skeleton hands reaching for me.

"Welcome home, my lady."

Slowly, a pleased smile curved my lips. "Thank you, Charon. I missed you."

CHAPTER SIX

MELANY

Thanks to his skull face that couldn't make facial expressions, I couldn't tell if the skeletal butler was happy to see me. You needed muscles and tissue to achieve that feat, but I assumed he did by the slight uptick in his voice. It wasn't nearly as creepy as usual.

"Did you miss me?" I asked him.

"Of course I did, my lady. It's been extra quiet here."

Cerberus took that moment to bark, as if disproving Charon's point. I scratched his heads again, then he loped out of the hall, wagging his tail.

I wasn't sure if Charon was telling me the truth or not about missing me. I supposed it really didn't matter. He didn't owe me anything. He wasn't *my* butler.

"Will you be staying, my lady? I could make up your old room for you."

Longing filled me, and I moved toward the closed door to Hades' room. "I was hoping I could stay in here." Pushing the door and walked into his chambers. Charon floated in behind me, the hem of his dark cloak dragging on the stone floor.

My heart leapt into my throat when I saw movement in the shadows, on the far side of the room, near the huge, canopied, king-sized bed. "Hades?" I murmured with hope, licking my dry lips.

A shape stepped out of the darkness. "He's dead, girl. Didn't you get the memo?" Her voice was just as shrill and high-pitched as I remembered. Megaera moved toward me, her small, blood red eyes narrowing. "I didn't think you'd come back. You are, after all, the hero of the war after defeating Zeus. I thought you'd settle at the academy with all your glory and fame."

Startled, I stepped back from the Fury. We'd trained together for months, and fought side by side during the war, but I still wasn't one hundred percent sure we were allies. I didn't really trust her, and with Hades gone, there was no reason she wouldn't rip my innards out and eat them for breakfast. I was certain he'd had to remind her several times during the months I'd live here that I wasn't on the menu.

"I would've been here sooner, but I couldn't get through the shadows to come back. I was blocked. Believe me, I tried every chance I got."

Megaera nodded, a tendril of stringy green hair falling over her prominent forehead. "Makes sense. Hades was the one who granted you entrance. And now that he's dead…"

I cringed every time she said it. I knew it to be true. I watched it happen. He died at my feet, protecting me from Zeus' lightning bolt, but I hated hearing it over and over again. I supposed I thought if I didn't say it, or hear it, then maybe there was hope that it wasn't true. That he was just playing possum, and would suddenly appear out of nowhere with a smile on his handsome face, a glint in his devilish eyes, and a story about how clever he was to have fooled everyone.

"How are *you* here then?" I glanced toward the door. "Are Allecto and Tisiphone here too?"

"They're sleeping in the rafters of the training room." She walked over to a table along one wall, where Hades kept decanters of wine, pouring herself a cup of something red. "We're here because we have our own connections to the underworld. Just like Charon and Cerberus. We were born out of the darkness. You, on the other hand, were just adopted."

Wine sloshed over the rim as Megaera gestured to me with the crystal glass, dripping onto the floor before she chugged down the drink. She wiped at her black lips with the back of her hand, and set the glass down with an audible clink.

I wasn't scared of her. Not anymore. When I came here a year ago, yeah, she and her bat-winged sisters frightened the crap out of me. Yet, I'd earned my scars honestly, through pain and torture. I earned my place here in the underworld and she knew it.

"I'm going to stay here."

Her eyebrow arched dubiously. "Says who?"

My scars lit up like a Christmas tree when I moved toward her, forcing her to shield her eyes from the glare. "Says me."

After taking a careful but noticeable step away from me, she shrugged. "Whatever. Stay as long as you want. It won't bring him back." And with that delightful parting remark, she left me alone in the room.

I wanted to shout after her, but it would've been pointless. Number one, she wouldn't care. Out of the three Fury sisters, Megaera was the snarkiest and the one I had mostly avoided in the past, when I could. And two, she wasn't wrong.

Movement behind me made me jump, and I swung around to see Charon floating patiently nearby. I'd forgotten he was there. "Shall I make a fire for you, my lady?" He gestured with skeletal fingers toward the large hearth.

I nodded. "Yes. Thank you, Charon. I'll stay in here for a couple of days, if that's all right with you?"

He bowed his bony head. "It is what Lord Hades would want."

I wasn't so sure about that, Hades hated it when I touched his things, but I smiled at him anyway. "Thanks."

Within seconds, a fire roared in the ornate hearth, and Charon left. Welcoming orange light filled the space, and I was able to make out some of the furniture, especially the four-poster bed at the far end of the room. Dark drapes were drawn around the frame, as if someone was tucked in for the night.

Memories of the night when I had a horrible dream about my friends and Lucian returned to me—I could still see the blood in my mind—and I had used the shadow ways to come here. I had moved to the bed, which had its drapes drawn, and yanked them aside to find Hades lying on top of the mattress, eyes closed, hands resting on his chest.

He'd looked dead then, like a vampire in his coffin. When he awoke, I demanded that he release me, and send me back to the academy. He did, but only because I'd been summoned to do some training there anyway.

A shaky hand reached for the drapes now, and slowly pulled them back, wishing with all my heart that I would find a sleeping, grumpy Hades on the bed—set to scold me for waking him—but the bed was empty as I knew it would be.

Crawling onto the mattress, I wrapped myself in the soft black blanket and brought the fabric to my nose, inhaling a deep breath. The scent of warm spices filled my nostrils, making my belly clench. It was his smell. One that I had come to covet over the months I'd trained here in his hall. I'd bugged him about wearing too much cologne, but secretly, I had loved it. I suspected he knew it and continued to do so. For me.

As I wrapped myself in his blankets, savoring the scent of him, I shut my eyes against the well of emotion, but let the tears come. Grabbing one of his pillows, I crushed it to my chest tightly, and sobbed until my whole body shook.

This was the release I needed. That I'd been craving ever since I watched Hades turn to dust in my arms. I hadn't had an opportunity to fall completely apart since the end of the war. I'd immediately been given responsibilities to teach and be a leader for others at the academy. The expectation to hold my shit together was intense, and with everyone watching me every second of every day—waiting for me to crack—I didn't feel like I could.

I needed to find my way here, to be around everything that reminded me of *him*, to rejoice in our time together, and grieve.

Holy shit, I needed to grieve.

The tears didn't seem to ease. I cried until I fell asleep, and when I woke, I was laying on my back in a field of yellow wildflowers. Sitting up, I saw that the land stretched on in every direction; I couldn't see the end of it. I'd been in this place before. When I drank poison at a gala at the school and died, I woke up here. In Elysium.

Knowing where I was going and what I was going to see, I got to my feet and walked west. Over the rise the valley, the land opened up with more flowers of every color ever made, and the narrow stream meandered through it like a serpent. Beyond that were several high rock formations, vines wrapping around the stone in an intimate hug. Waterfalls cascaded down all sides, forming white foam at the bottom.

On top of the highest rock cliff, was a white stone temple. It was there that I met Persephone, and saw my parents for the first time since their death six years ago. I'd had no idea that they'd been involved with the academy until I saw their picture in a book about it. They'd been recruits way before I was born, and my mother had suggested that their car accident hadn't been an accident. I still didn't know if that was true or not.

The first time I mounted the steps to the temple, I was overwrought with fear. Now, I felt anticipation, and a tiny tendril of hope blossomed in my chest.

When I passed between the two massive pillars and entered that holy place, my heart raced. I walked toward the large stone fountain of a siren sitting on a bed of rocks, water gushing out of her mouth and up into the air. I stood there and looked around, checking every shadow in every corner. There was no sound but the burbling of the fountain. It seemed I was alone.

Nevertheless, I'd come here for a reason. I didn't think I had died in my sleep, so this might've been only a dream. Or it wasn't, and someone had called me to Elysium.

"Hades?" I whispered, but my voice echoed through the temple regardless.

"He's not here."

Whipping around, I came face to face with a beautiful woman of long black hair, and dark eyes. Her lips were as red as blood, and her eyelids and cheeks sparkled with gold flecks as if she'd been dipped in glitter. Persephone looked just as I remembered her. Pale and perfect.

Her lips curved with a smile. "I didn't think to see you again so soon, Melany."

"I didn't think I'd be here either. I'm supposed to be asleep in…"

"Hades' bed?"

My cheeks flushed. Was she jealous? Long ago, she'd lived with Hades in his hall. She'd been his lover back then, and I suspected she still loved him. We had that in common.

"Why am I here? Who called me?"

"I don't know. Maybe you *are* just dreaming."

Reaching out, I touched her arm. She felt plenty real to me. "This doesn't feel like a dream."

Her hand took mine, and she spun me around as if we were waltzing. "Are you sure about that?"

I pulled away from her. I didn't want her confusing me, and Persephone had that way about her. She was seductive. "If this is where Gods and demigods come when they die, then why isn't Hades here?"

With a simple shrug, the Goddess continued her

dancing around as if she hadn't a care in the world. I supposed she didn't, considering she was dead and living in this heavenly world. Still, I had questions, and I needed answers.

"He's not on Earth either. So, where is he?"

LUCIAN

"I don't know what else to do for her." Chiron's hooves clicked on the marble floor as he moved around the infirmary, making sure he was stocked up on supplies like bandages and herbal tinctures. Accidents happened during training, and he needed to be prepared. "The sessions we have don't seem to be working. In fact, I think they're just making it worse on her. During our last meeting, she cracked the wall." He pointed to a section of the infirmary where I saw there was indeed a large crack from ceiling to floor.

"There has to be a way to help her control the

power inside of her." I ran both hands through my hair, feeling impotent and useless.

After I flew to the academy, I had come straight to the infirmary to talk to the centaur healer. I believed in his abilities; I'd seen him bring people back from the dead. I was sure he could do something for Melany. If he couldn't, then I didn't know who could.

He gave me a sympathetic look. "Maybe we should talk to Apollo. He can access the mind. With his help, we might be able to construct a protective shield inside Melany's mind, so that the power swirling through her body can't hurt her."

Or anyone else, I thought, nodding. "At this point, I think anything is worth a try."

"I'll talk to him. Come to see me tomorrow. I should have an answer one way or another."

Intending to find Jasmine, Georgina and Ren, I left the infirmary. Maybe together, we could come up with some plan to help Melany. As I walked through the halls, I suspected Jasmine was out on the field, training with Athena. She'd lost her fire power, but she had only improved with the bow.

Georgina was probably with Demeter either outside in the garden, or inside Demeter's Hall tending to the plants. She'd lost her earth power but she still liked to garden. I suspected it was because she was hoping that by trying extra hard she could get it back, and no one had the heart to tell her that it didn't work that way. Although Ren had lost his water ability, he was still an expert swimmer, and on most days he could be found at the lake.

I'd grab Jasmine first; she was the closest right now.

The large staircase took me down to the main entrance of the academy. I needed to cross another wing, then I could use the rear doors to the training field. As I came around the corner to the main corridor that led to the dining hall, I nearly collided with a girl of long, curly, strawberry blond hair. She just stood in the middle of the corridor, facing one of the walls. I didn't recognize her. She must've been one of the new recruits, but I was pretty sure she wasn't supposed to be in this part of the academy, since Prometheus was still taking the group for a tour of the grounds.

"Hey," I called to her.

She didn't flinch or speak.

"Are you lost?" I reached out to touch her shoulder, trying hard not to startle her.

Slowly, she turned around, and I nearly stumbled backward when she glanced at me. Her eyes were a dark green, like an emerald. I'd never seen eyes like that, yet it was the way they seemed to look right through me that filled me with unease… as if I wasn't even there. I swore to the Gods she never even blinked. It was rather spooky, and unnerving.

"Are you one of the new recruits?"

The girl didn't answer. She just kept staring at me —well, through me—causing me to suppress a shudder.

Not knowing what else to do, I snapped my fingers in front of her face, and that seemed to wake her.

Her brow furrowed, her dazed gaze finally seeming to focus. "Where am I?"

"You're in the west wing. Are you supposed to be here?"

"I don't know."

"Okay. Tell you what, I'll lead you back to the group. I'm pretty sure they are still out on the grounds."

Unable to say anything else, she just licked her lips, green eyes narrowing on me.

"I'm Lucian. What's your name?"

"Cassandra."

"Nice to meet you, Cassandra. Where are you from?"

"Kios."

I nodded. "I know a few people from Kios."

She continued to stare at me as she gave me one-word answers.

"Okay." I gestured to the hall. "How about we go this way, and I'll get you back to the group." I didn't want to be around this girl any longer, but I also couldn't just let her wander around the academy unchaperoned.

Cassandra turned with me to walk down the hall, but suddenly grabbed my arm harshly. Her eyelids fluttered, eyes literally rolling back into her head until there was nothing but white. My first reaction was to pull away from her, but I soon realized her body was starting to convulse. I helped her to the floor, putting my hand behind her head so she didn't smash it on the stone tiles as she seized.

Watching her convulse made me sick to my stomach, yet I didn't know what else to do. I couldn't cry out for help as the halls were empty, and the rooms beyond them closed. I guessed all I could do for her, was ride it out and make sure she didn't hurt herself.

As quick as she started to shake, she instantly stopped, but her eyes were still white as her eyelids fluttered. Her left hand grasped onto my other arm, and though her mouth opened to speak, nothing came out.

"Cassandra? Can you hear me?"

And then everything went blank for me.

A moment later, I found myself sitting on my ass on the tiled floor of the west wing corridor, a few feet away from the red-headed girl. She finally sat up, blinking at me, and I noticed her eyes were back to normal.

Her brow furrowed with confusion. "Where am I?"

Feeling very muddled, I shook my head. A second ago I had been holding onto Cassandra while she had a seizure, and afterward everything had gone blank. Not dark, like I had passed out, but empty. I couldn't remember how I got from touching her, to sitting a few feet away. How had that happened?

Standing, I reached down to helped her. "We're in the west wing of the academy."

She chewed on her lips, still frowning. "How did I get here?"

"To be honest, I don't know. I found you here in the hallway."

"Did I pass out or something?" Her hand rubbed her head absentmindedly.

Frowning, and just as confused, I shrugged. "I'm not sure."

"Why were we both on the floor?"

"I wish I knew." I stared at her. She'd had a seizure, hadn't she? That's what happened, right? She convulsed and I helped her lie on the floor until she stopped.

"Who are you?" she asked.

"I'm Lucian, remember? And you're Cassandra, from Kios."

She nodded, her lips twitching up into a shy smile. It made me smile in return. She was cute, with her bright green eyes, and the smattering of freckles over the bridge of her nose and cheeks. She was tiny too, could easily fit into the crook of my arm. Not that I was thinking about putting her in there.

"I'll help you get back to the group."

"Thank you. I appreciate it."

We walked together down the hall while I prattled on about the different paintings we passed along the way—more out of nerves than anything else. I wasn't exactly sure why this girl made me nervous, but she did. I'd had goose flesh all over my body since first running into her, and it wasn't going away.

Something significant had happened between us. I knew it with every fiber of my being, but I just couldn't remember. It was like waking from a bad dream, with only the feeling of dread creeping on your skin.

A bad dream.

That was what it had felt like. I'd had my fair share of unsettling dreams while being at the academy, especially after the battle. Sometimes I would wake in a cold sweat, my hands trembling. I supposed it was like having PTSD, like some people suffered. Not that this feeling was the same, it just felt akin to experiencing something life-altering. I didn't know what it was, I couldn't really identify what I was sensing, so I tried to push it from my mind.

Instead, I concentrated on getting Cassandra back to where she belonged. That was easier to wrap my mind around right now.

CHAPTER EIGHT

MELANY

I continued to watch as Persephone danced around the stone water fountain, her white robe swirling around her legs. It was as if she was mocking me and my concerns, which only made my anger rise to a boiling point with each passing second. I didn't think she was telling me the truth about Hades. He died. I'd seen him die, so he had to have come to Elysium. Maybe she was jealous of the relationship we'd developed and was keeping me from him. Keeping him all to herself.

"Where is he, Persephone?"

The Goddess stopped spinning and looked at me.

"Do you think I have him tucked away in some secret corner, Melany?" Her laughter irked me even more. "You really don't know Hades if you think I could have any sway on him or tell him what to do. He is his own man and does what he wants. Even in death."

She was right, of course. I just didn't want to hear it. My grief had manufactured into so much anger that all I could see was red. I was beyond the point of rational thought. "Then, you won't mind if I just go take a look myself."

Whirling around with purpose, I stomped across the white marble floor to the other open door at the far side of the temple. Green pastures and sunshine extended beyond the tall stone pillars. I heard Persephone sigh loudly as I moved past her, my fists clenched at my sides.

The closer I got to the open door the more I could see the sun and hear the birds. It was true what was written about Elysium; it was a paradise with no bad weather, and endless amounts of delicious food and drink, fields of wildflowers and fruit-bearing trees. Who wouldn't want to spend their eternal death here?

For a brief second, I saw a shimmer in the air around the arch of the exit as I neared it, but I didn't think much of it. Taking a big step to go through the door, I ran into something solid, and was forced backward. I rubbed at my nose, as it stung from the bump. For sure, I thought it was going to bleed; it hurt so much from the impact.

I wondered if I'd walked into the doorframe by accident. Maybe I'd been so distracted by the turmoil inside me that I didn't look where I was going. Slowly, I took a few steps forward and reached out toward the space between the pillars. My hand came up against something solid. It was like glass or see through plastic, yet not like that at all. It felt strange against my skin, like sticking my hand into a buzzing, vibrating beehive.

"What's with the forcefield?" I asked, looking over my shoulder at Persephone, who was lounging on a sofa while causally eating grapes from a bushel.

"You're not dead, so you can't move past this temple." She waved a hand in the air. "It's like the train station, but you don't have a ticket to get on the train."

Disappointment coursed through me, and I stepped away from the door, joining her at the sofa. "If it's like you said, and I'm dreaming, then I should be able to go wherever I want."

A wry smile curved her lips as her eyebrow arched. "You should know by now, Melany, that dreams and reality can merge together, and you don't have any control over that at all." She offered me some grapes.

With a shake of my head, I sat on the edge of the sofa. "Why am I here then?"

Persephone shrugged. "I don't know this time around. I was as surprised to see you, as you were to wake up here."

"Can I see my parents again?"

"No. They are where they need to be. Last time, I knew you were coming, and I planned for them to be here so you could talk to them and understand what had happened in the past." Eating some more fruit, she observed me, then her expression changed. Frowning, she sat up, and it looked like she was choking.

Swiftly reaching over, I patted her back—like my mom had done for me once, when I'd choked on a piece of chicken—but Persephone slapped my arm away, shaking her head. A frightened look took over her face when she turned to glance at me. My stomach churned in response. Something was going on, but I didn't know what.

I could feel a presence in the air, or in a way, it was more of a lack of something. Like a void. An emptiness that surrounded us on the sofa.

"Get away!" she shouted.

I jumped to my feet, although I was unsure if she was talking to me or not. Although, she wasn't looking at me when she yelled, but into the vacant room.

"Are you okay?"

A few fat purple orbs fell from her hands, rolling across the marble tiles as Persephone started to tremble. Except, it wasn't so much a shiver, her whole body was quivering like a tuning fork. Horror-struck, she looked at me, her eyes beseeching me to help her, but I had no idea what was happening to her.

The Goddess' mouth opened and closed, gulping for oxygen like a fish out of water. She reached a hand up to me, it was shaking so badly that at one point it blurred. I could see it, then I couldn't. It was as if the very molecules that made up her body were dancing.

"I-I… can't… something's wrong…" Even her voice vibrated with each word.

Panicked, I just watched her. I didn't know what to do. I had no idea how to help her because I wasn't sure what was happening to her. Despite being around a bunch of magical Gods for the past year or so, I'd never seen anything like this.

"What should I do? How can I help you?"

Squeezing her eyes shut, she tucked her arms into her sides, like she was trying to hold herself together. It worked. Her form stopped violently shaking for a moment.

"My lifeline… I can feel it moving."

I frowned. "What does that mean?"

"Our lives are but threads, weaved by…"

She started to oscillate again. This time it was her entire body, moving so quickly that she flickered in and out of my vision.

"What does that mean?"

"…sisters… out of time… Thanatos… ask… save…"

Persephone's image wavered before my eyes, like a radio broadcast trying to tune in on some static-filled station. My flesh crawled as bits and pieces of her vanished from sight, until the only thing left floating in the air were her dark, intense eyes. It was unsettling to watch, and I had to fight not to drop to my knees and retch. Finally, her eyes slowly dissolved, like ash into water.

"Persephone?!" I whipped around, looking in every corner of the temple. Jogging in a circle, I searched for her everywhere, all the way around the fountain, peering into every crevice and alcove. "Persephone?!"

I was completely alone. I walked to the pillars again and tested it, yet I couldn't break through the barrier. The sun still shone, and I could hear the birds chirping, so that hadn't been altered.

Going out the door through which I'd entered, I left the temple, walking to the edge of the cliff. I peered out over the vast, tranquil valley, but all I could see was the stream I'd crossed, and beyond that, the sweeping fields of yellow wildflowers that seemed to go on forever. I was absolutely alone.

"Persephone?!" I called for her once more. My voice floated on the breeze, vanishing among the rocks.

What was I supposed to do now?

Before the Goddess disappeared, she said something about Thanatos. It triggered me to remember the cryptic thing he'd told me when I'd saved that man's life on the docks.

"I have no thread for this man… It means this mortal won't die, even though it is his time."

Persephone too had mentioned something about time and threads. Obviously, whatever had happened to her was connected to Thanatos in some way. I needed to talk to him.

But first, I needed to wake the hell up.

Leaning over the edge of the cliff, I swallowed, feeling my stomach do a few somersaults. It was one hell of a long trip down, but it was my only way out of here. Mind you, when Persephone had pushed me off the cliff last time I visited, it had catapulted me out of my death. What would happen this time?

I supposed there was only one way to find out the answer. Victory didn't favor cowards.

Swallowing, I closed my eyes, and jumped off the

cliff—surprised my heart didn't explode from the fear coursing through my body.

I didn't remember screaming when I leapt off the edge, but I must have, because a second later I found myself laying on the floor next to the bed in Hades' room, screaming my head off. I immediately snapped my lips shut, embarrassed, pulse still raising from the adrenaline of the fall. Jumping to my feet, I side-stepped, I was a bit woozy—not surprising, considering what I'd been through just now. My head actually hurt, and I wondered if I hit it on the nightstand when I rolled out of bed.

Rubbing at the sore spot near my right temple, I left the room, in search of someone to ask about Thanatos and how I could talk to him. When I opened the door to the training room and walked in, it felt like wandering into the lion's den with a piece of fresh meat wrapped around my throat, but it had to be done.

It was pitch dark inside, and I nearly tripped over something on the floor. A ball of fire formed between my hands, allowing me to see one of the wooden combat dummies in my path. After stepping over it, I carried the fireball like a flashlight to illuminate my way into the cavernous room.

The rustling sound of wood creaking reached me from above—the Furies must have been waking. I really hoped they weren't angry that I'd woken them, or this might be the shortest quest for information I'd ever performed. Even though I wasn't afraid of them anymore, it didn't mean I was an idiot, and didn't think they'd hurt me if they could.

"I like the sound of your screams." A raspy voice came from behind me. "Scared of the shadows now that Hades isn't around to protect you?"

I whipped around to find Tisiphone hovering in the air, slightly above my head.

"I'm sorry I woke you, but I need to ask you something."

Slowly, she lowered herself to the ground, folding her bat wings behind her wide back. Tisiphone was a few inches taller than Megaera, with the same blood red eyes and crimson stains along her cheeks, so she was just as intimidating. A bit more actually, but she'd always been kinder to me. We'd even had a few laughs over the past year. Out of all the Furies, she was the one with a sense of humor. Albeit a morbid one sometimes, but still, she liked to laugh and joke around, so out of all of the sisters, I was relieved I'd woken her and not the others.

"What do you want to ask, little Bo Peep? I bet you taste like sheep." Her darkened tongue swept her black lips, and I had to suppress a shudder of revulsion.

I guessed we weren't as friendly as I thought we'd been.

"How do I find Thanatos? I need to talk to him."

Her eyes widened with pleasant surprise. "You wish to speak with the God of Death?" A morbid grin stretched her features and I instantly paled, regretting my choice of words. It was obviously the wrong question to ask a demigod associated with blood, vengeance, and destruction.

Tisiphone took a step toward me, and I moved backward. She took another step, and I did too, until I ended up hitting something solid.

Arms came around me, and a knife pressed against my throat. "We thought you'd never ask."

CHAPTER NINE

MELANY

There was no doubt it was Megaera who held me from behind, her dagger pressed to my throat. Allecto was much bigger and stronger than either of her sisters. She wouldn't need a knife to rip open my skin. Besides that, Allecto wasn't one to play games, like the other two.

The blade nicked my skin when I struggled a little against her hold, and I could feel the trickle of blood slowly rolling down my neck. I wanted to believe they wouldn't kill me, but with Hades gone, I wasn't so sure —he'd been my protective shield. The Furies weren't known to have friends. Only enemies and victims. I was okay with being an enemy, I had lots of those, but I refused to be a victim.

"I would let me go if I were you," I warned, with more bravado than I was currently feeling.

Megaera snickered. "Not happening."

Leaning in, Tisiphone got in my face. "You talk tough for a scared little girl."

"Oh, I'm not scared." I smirked. "And I'm not a little girl."

"Yes, Hades saw to that, I'm sure." Megaera pressed the knife in harder. If I moved wrong, the blade would slice me deeply. Maybe too deep to heal.

"Jealous, Meg?" I quipped, knowing that was exactly the problem. She was the personification of jealousy. Everything she did was in response to some form of envious spite.

Tisiphone' laugh danced around us. "She got you there."

While the two of them bantered, I reached deep inside for every reserve of power I had—and I had tons to draw from thanks to my friends, who'd sacrificed their individual abilities to me so I could save the world. I was surprised the Furies couldn't feel it humming along my skin. I did. Twenty-four hours a day.

All the fire and lightning inside me—they would do the most damage—rose to the surface, hovering there just on the edge, ready for me to unleash it. I could taste it on my tongue. It tasted like ash and ruin, but I didn't have any other choice. They weren't giving me one.

"I'll give you one last chance to let me go," I challenged.

Tisiphone looked me over; I could see she was reconsidering their move. Maybe she saw the boiling power humming along my body, but Megaera wasn't playing.

More rivulets of blood trickled down my throat while she pressed the knife a little deeper, a little closer to my main artery. "Not going to happen. I'm going to have my—"

I didn't let her finish.

What seemed like a small bomb went off as I let loose everything inside me.

Both Tisiphone and Megaera were blown backward, no less than ten feet in either direction. The stench of burnt hair and flesh filled the room. It burned my nostrils as I stood there, quaking from the release of power. It was almost sexual with how it made my body and mind feel. I knew I should've been ashamed of that response, but I was past the point of caring about pleasantries.

Taking a deep breath, I let it out slowly, and the

remnants of flames snuffed out of my fingertips. Lightning still coiled along my body, following the lines of my many scars. I probably looked like one of those static electricity balls. The energy of it lit up the room.

Tisiphone and Megaera's grunts of pain echoed in the training room while they moved on the floor, both likely trying to gauge their injuries, which I suspected were plenty. I'd lessened the blow toward Tisiphone, but I'd definitely given the green-haired Fury my full attention. She deserved it.

"You fucking bitch!" Megaera managed to shriek. "You burned off my wings."

Facing her, I saw she was right. Where there had once been large fearsome leathery wings jutting out of her back, were now a few broken pieces of cartilage and melted membranes hanging grotesquely from her singed body.

"I warned you to let me go," I reminded with a bit of an arrogant smirk. "Twice."

Megaera had the nerve to stumble toward me, her hand raised menacingly. Her dagger had been fused with the skin of her palm from the heat of my blast. "I'm going to kill you!"

Before she could reach me though, Allecto jumped from the rafters and landed right between us, effectively cutting off her sister. "Stop," she growled. "Haven't you had enough, Sister?"

"Look what she did to me!" Megaera splayed out her arms to show that her clothes had been burned off, and her skin signed to black. All her green hair was gone, just a few tendrils still remained hanging along her face.

However, the worst of it was her chest. It had been scorched so badly that I could see her flesh and ribs beyond the torn flesh. My stomach roiled in response. How could a body sustain that much damage and still function? How could Megaera still be alive? I hadn't planned to kill her, but with that amount of fire power coming out of me, it should have.

"Quit whining," Allecto snapped. "It was self defense. You were going to slice open her neck." She gestured toward Tisiphone who had stumbled closer, her wings also burnt but not anywhere near the level of Megaera's injuries. "You don't hear Tis bitching about it."

Megaera gave off one final shriek of frustration and anger, then stomped out of the room.

"Go see if Charon has any ointment," Tisiphone called after her, then sat down on the floor with an audible grunt of pain. I was thankful that she seemed to accept that what had happened was fair play between us.

My body still sparkled like a live wire, but I wasn't bursting at the seams any longer. Still, Allecto took a distancing, respectful, step away from me. She was the smart one out of the sisters.

"So, you still have your friends' powers."

I sighed. "Yup. I've been trying to give them back but so far, no joy."

"Does it hurt?" Allecto asked.

"Every day."

She nodded, as if that gave her some sort of satisfaction, then licked her black lips. "Why do you need to talk to Thanatos?"

"Something's going on topside and in Elysium."

Her eyebrows lifted. "Elysium? You went there?"

"In my dreams. At least I think they were dreams. I don't know anymore." Exhaustion started to creep in, and I rubbed a hand over my face, but I was afraid to go back to sleep. "I don't really know what's going on, but twice now, I've heard the words threads and time. And it was suggested to me that Thanatos might have some answers."

Allecto glanced at Tisiphone. Something, some kind of knowing exchange passed between them. "Normally, I would tell you to travel along the river Styx, past the Asphodel Meadows and Mourning Fields, to the entrance of the Cave of Sorrow to find Thanatos, but I've heard that he's not been there for some time now."

My brows deeply creased. "I take it that's not normal."

"Gods no, that's not normal." Allecto's fire-red ponytail swung with the shake of her head. "Thanatos usually mopes around his little cave until he needs to pop out and grab a soul or two. But now he's supposedly not there at all."

"I saw him a couple days ago, topside, when some guy nearby had a heart attack. I went to help the man, but honestly, it didn't take much. He was dead, or should've been, and Thanatos showed up, but he didn't take the soul. The man just sat up like nothing had happened."

Allecto's frown deepened. She wandered over to the weapons' wall and pulled a bo staff down from it, twirling it around in her hands. I could tell that she was thinking, and the action helped her. It was her fidget spinner.

"We could talk to Hypnos, to see if he's seen his brother," Tisiphone suggested.

"Who is Hypnos?" I asked.

"The God of Sleep, duh." She shook her head.

"Where can I find him?"

"We'll go talk to him. You should leave the underworld," Allecto interjected.

"No. I'm not leaving."

"You came to find Hades. He's not here, as you have seen," she retorted. "You'll be safer topside, back at the academy."

"I'm not scared of—"

Spinning the bo staff over my head, she rested it along my shoulder. "Megaera will get her revenge. Believe me."

I swallowed. I did believe her, as she was the epitome of vengeance. She knew more than anyone else the levels mortals, demigods, and Gods went to get retribution.

"Neither Tis or I will be able to stop her now."

"I can protect myself." I lifted my chin.

"Obviously," Tisiphone sneered.

"But that's no way to live, Melany," Allecto reminded. "Trust me, I know. You are better off at the academy. After we talk to Hypnos, we will let you know what he says."

"Besides," Tisiphone added, "If Thanatos isn't here, he's somewhere up top, wandering the lands." She chuckled. "Reminds me of The Black Death.

During that time, Thanatos never came back home. He was much too busy."

My chest grew tight at the thought. Was that what was happening? He was preparing for a global plague? I shook my head. That couldn't be it.

"Fine, I'll go back, but I want to know immediately what Hypnos said about Thanatos."

"Sure thing, mistress Melany." Tisiphone snorted.

"If Thanatos is wandering around, how do I find him?" I asked.

Tisiphone got to her feet, stumbling for a moment but steadied herself. I almost felt bad for injuring her. Almost. She had been intent on killing me, so I did what I had to do to protect myself.

"You find him, like any normal person does." She grinned at me. Half her upper lip was missing and her teeth poked through it. It was grotesque, making me want to look away. "You die."

Allecto's staff spun around again, nearly hitting me with the tip. "Or you kill a bunch of people. Either way you'll get his attention."

"I'm not killing anyone. I'm not a monster"

"It hasn't stopped you before." Tisiphone made a face. "I remember you killing a few people during the war. Like that dark-haired girl. What was her name? Revana?"

My scars flared up as a mixture of anger and sorrow filled me. Revana's death was one of many of my regrets. "I didn't kill her."

Tisiphone squinted from the white glare and shrugged, her shoulder looked dislocated. "Sure, little girl. Whatever you tell yourself to muddle through the day."

"Whatever. I'm done talking to you." I closed my hand, snuffing out the fire that I'd subconsciously started in my palm, and moved toward the door.

"See you later," Tisiphone called after me, hers and Allecto's laughter trailing after me.

I decided to take their advice and leave the underworld... for the time being. I'd be back once Megaera calmed down and didn't want to rip out my innards to eat them. Although I wasn't entirely sure that time would ever come.

To be safe, I'd leave and return to the academy. I didn't find what I was looking for, there weren't any answers for me down here, at least not right now.

On the way out, I ran into Charon. "I've got to go, Charon, but I'll be back."

He reached for me, wrapping his skeletal fingers around my wrist, but I was pretty sure it was a gesture of kindness and not a threat. He tugged me a little closer to him. "When you're ready, this place will be waiting," he whispered in my ear. "Lord Hades always meant it to be yours."

Eyes widening, I gaped at him. There was no way that was true. I couldn't possibly be the mistress of the underworld. Yet deep down inside, I felt a spark of joy. Happiness. Something I hadn't thought I deserved. Maybe this was always where I was meant to be.

CHAPTER TEN

LUCIAN

I stood in darkness alone, confused. It was how a lot of my dreams started. Followed by me walking into a scene from a memory. Most times it was of the battle, but sometimes, as a reward, it was of a moment between Melany and me.

This time, however, a voice came out of the shadows. I couldn't tell if it was male or female. It just resounded around me with force. Power. Compulsion.

"Look!" the voice shouted. "See!"

"See what?!" I was about to shout in return, when a quick series of images flooded my mind. Nothing I could fully discern. Just quick snippets of brightly lit rooms, green fields, wildflowers. It was like scrolling through photos on a cell phone. It was going so fast that my stomach churned. Nausea enveloped me and I thought I was going to throw up. Suddenly, the images stop moving, and one completely encompassed me. So much so, that I was transported there, and was now in a vivid dreamscape.

Everything around me was bright. Warm sunshine poured over me, and the stone bench I sat on inside a lush garden. At first, I thought it was the garden here at the academy, but it was bigger, denser, prettier. The sky above was as blue as a robin's egg, just like it was at the academy, but here it seemed bluer, brighter, more vivid. There were clouds, yet they weren't above in the sky but floating below me.

I sensed I was waiting for something, or someone. The flutter of anticipation filled my stomach and I nervously ran my hand over the cotton of the beige pants I wore. I wasn't alone, not really. There was movement around me, but I couldn't quite make out the shapes of those nearby. Their laughter reached me though, their happy voices—both male and female.

When a form came out from the large white and gold temple near me, I got to my feet. That was who I'd been waiting for. I knew it deep down in my gut. I felt the smile blossoming on my face as the person came into view. It was a tall man, with golden waves not unlike my own. He too smiled.

"Owen," I greeted.

My brother embraced me, patting me on the back. "Baby bro. I'm so happy to see you again."

It had been over four years since I'd seen my older brother, because he'd been called to the academy four years before I had. My family hadn't heard from him again, which was how it went for those recruited into the Gods' Army. When you answered the call, you agreed to give everything up, including your family—or that was how it worked when Zeus was in power. Although, I wasn't sure if that was going to change now that Prometheus was at the head of the academy again.

Owen pulled back, and looked me over. "You've gotten muscles."

Laughing, I pushed him. "I've always had muscles, you ass."

"Yeah, but not as big as mine." He flexed his large bicep like an idiot. He'd been doing that ever since he hit puberty at fourteen.

Gods, I missed him. I hadn't realized how much until this moment.

After lowering his arm, he looked around, and his expression changed. It got hard, serious. Taking a hold of me, he pulled me out of the garden, and into a shadowed area near a copse of vast olive trees. A vulture squawked from a nearby tree, followed by the bleat of a couple of baby goats.

"What are you doing here, Lucian?"

I frowned. "I'm here to see you. Prometheus let us come to Olympus. It's part of our final training."

"You can't be here, Brother. It's too dangerous."

"What? Why? I don't understand."

"I can't explain it, but there's something wrong with time in this place. It may only feel like an hour here, but it could be years down on earth."

With his statement, I remembered Melany saying something to me about time when she was in the underworld. A few days for her had been a few weeks for me at the academy.

"You need to go back." Urgency filled his eyes, and he grabbed both my arms. "There's something wrong with all of it. Something's broken. Humanity needs you to fix it."

"I don't understand."

"You will... find *her*... She will help you..."

His voice trailed off, and I had trouble seeing him. It looked like he was fading, dissipating into mist. I reached for him, but my hands only grasped the fog.

"Owen!"

I jolted out of sleep, and sat ramrod straight in my

cot. My heart thundered against my ribcage, making it hard to breathe. I sat there, staring into the darkness of my room, trying to calm my body and mind.

It had only been a dream. That was all. As I repeated that mantra in my mind, the vivid images in my head started to fade a little. I hadn't thought about my brother, Owen, in years. Not since he left home to come train for the Gods' Army. When I was called, I assumed we would've been reunited, but that hadn't happened.

Until now?

I shook my head. No, it was a dream. It hadn't been real.

My startled gaze dropped to my hands, sure that my fingers had touched him when he hugged me. I could still feel the remnants of his brotherly embrace on my chest and back, where he had patted me. The tickle of his hair against my cheek had seemed so damn real.

Licking my lips, I noticed my throat was also dry, as if I'd been shouting. I swung my legs over my cot and set them firmly on the floor, hoping the feel of the cool tiles would ground me. It did a little so I stood, walking to the closet, and sliding on a new pair of sweatpants and a T-shirt. The ones I'd slept in were damp with sweat.

Despite the late hour, I felt awake and restless. I didn't think I'd get any more sleep than I'd had already. The experience clung to me like prickly vines, and I was having trouble shaking it off. It was the most vivid dream I'd ever had. It felt more like a memory than something conjured from my subconscious.

Sliding open the window in my room, I climbed up onto the sill to overlook the lands of the academy. My room was in Zeus' Hall, so it sat high up, several stories above the ground in the tallest tower.

Inhaling a deep breath of cool, early morning air, I dove off the ledge, feeling my wings shoot out of my back as I plummeted to the earth. Much like a parachute, they slowed my descent, until I flapped them a few times and rose back into the sky. Out of all the powers I'd developed here, flying was my number one love. Nothing felt as invigorating, more freeing, then soaring through the open air on your own steam, the wind blowing on your face and through your hair. It was perfection.

I flew up over the spires, swooping down toward the woods and lake, its dark waters a large, black ink blot on the ground. The area around it had become a place of solace for me over the past year. It was also where Melany and I had gone several times when we wanted to be alone. Thoughts of her entered my mind as I touched down on the rocky shore, wondering where she had gone off too again. You'd think after this long I'd be used to her sudden disappearances, but they still sucked.

They hurt too, even though it was arrogant to think they had anything to do with me.

Picking up a couple of stones I skipped them along the lake's tranquil, glass-like surface. My record so far was only four skips, though Melany always beat me with at least five. Once, she got seven skips. I was pretty sure that was a world record or something.

"You don't hold the rock right."

The unexpected voice made me whirl around to find Melany walking out of the woods; a swath of moonlight lit up her face and hair. In her dark clothes, with her black wings, she lived up to the name of Dark Angel of Pecunia. Although she'd hate to hear it.

My first instinct was to go to her, wrap her in my arms and kiss her. She'd been gone a few days, but if she was where I'd thought she'd gone, it would've only been a night for her. So, I refrained, knowing she wouldn't appreciate my neediness for her. I hated how we had parted and I wanted to mend things with her, but that had been her problem with me. My tendency to bow to her every whim. This time I wouldn't bend. I would stand here and pretend it didn't matter, that I hadn't been hurting while she'd been gone, even if it was killing me.

"Sure I do." Determined, and glad she was back, I curled my index finger around the side of the flat rock, showed her, then flung it out over the water. The stone touched the surface four times, making a plinking sound, then sunk. I groaned.

Chuckling, Melany picked up a flat rock from the ground, curled her fingers around it and flung it, snapping her wrist. The rock skipped across the water six times. She turned to me and took a bow.

Laughter escaped me. I hadn't seen her this light-hearted in months. It was nice.

"What are you doing out here?" she asked.

"I couldn't sleep." I eyed her curiously. "How about you?"

She shook her head. "I wonder if that's just how it will be for us forever."

I shrugged. "I don't know. I hope not. I used to love to sleep in."

"Me too. Some days I would sleep so long that Sophia would check in on me to make sure I was still breathing." Her face darkened a bit with the memory of her adoptive mother, but I was glad that she talked about her. She needed to, she bottled too much inside of her.

It wasn't only her powers that were bubbling at the surface, waiting to explode.

Turning to the side so she couldn't see my face, I threw another rock across the lake. "Where did you go?"

"The underworld."

"I thought all the portals were closed to you."

"They are, but I found another way in." Melany gestured to the trees, and I knew what she meant.

"You saw Hecate? I thought her tree had been destroyed."

"Her tree is gone, but I found a way through the stump, and reached the underground tunnel you told me about." She shrugged. "I didn't see Hecate though. She must not be around anymore."

I nodded. I hoped the witch found another tree to inhabit. Like many of the Gods in this realm she was born to darkness, but she wasn't malicious. She'd helped me when I went looking for Melany, and she'd fought with us in the war against Zeus. Hecate had paid a price for that, like we all had.

"Did you find what you were looking for?"

"I don't know. Sort of. I saw Cerberus, Charon, and the Furies. They're all still living in the hall."

"How were they?"

"Angry, vengeful, impossible to deal with. So, the usual."

A soft laugh rumbled in my chest, but there was still one thing I really needed to know. "Was it worth it going down there? Do you feel better?"

Her shoulders swiftly rose and fell. "I don't know. To be honest, Lucian, I'm not sure I'll ever feel better. What's that supposed to mean, even? Better than what?"

I didn't answer, mostly because I didn't know what to say to that. I wasn't sure there was even an answer.

"Hungry?" My gaze lifted to the pinkened sky. "The caf should be serving breakfast by now."

She nodded. "I could go for some pancakes."

I reached out my hand to her and with a soft smile, she took it. We flapped our wings, slowly rising into the air together. Her smile suddenly turned into a wicked grin. "Race you!" She was off like a shot.

Swirling in the air, I had to work extra hard to catch up to her, but when I did, it was like old times. We swooped around each other, taunting and teasing the other, and my heart swelled with a hope I hadn't felt in a long time.

I knew it wouldn't last, but for now, it was enough.

CHAPTER ELEVEN

MELANY

After eating a huge stack of pancakes with syrup and whipped cream in Lucian's company, I felt like I could get through the next few days. It was just us in the dining hall, and it had felt great.

However, now that the new recruits were here, I had a job to do. We all did.

Lucian was teaching hand-to-hand combat alongside Heracles. Jasmine was helping Artemis with bow lessons. Georgina was working with Demeter in the gardens, to help supply herbs to both Chiron for healing, and Dionysus for his radical potions and tinctures. Despite not having his water powers, Ren still possessed expert sword handling so he was helping Athena teach weapons training, since Ares no longer taught at the academy and was locked away with Aphrodite in Tartarus.

I was on my way across the academy grounds to the separate building where the elementals were taught. Because I had destroyed Zeus, they thought I would be the best person to teach how to create, handle, and manipulate lightning, since none of the other Gods had an affinity to it.

Technically, the cyclopes could control lightning too, and in particular, Brontes, the eldest of the giant beings, had created Zeus's lightning bolt for him. The issue was, Prometheus thought Brontes was much too big, standing at ten feet or so, and didn't really speak much to be able to train the students. So, it was left up to me. I wasn't convinced I was the best person to teach anyone anything to be honest, especially not in my chaotic state.

The large stone structure stood tall as I stepped inside, and was immediately greeted by inquisitive stares. It seemed that the other four instructors—Poseidon, Hephaistos, Demeter, and Erebus—had been having a little meeting about me and my ability to give this class.

"Hey, Melany," Demeter welcomed with a head nod.

"Hey." I gestured to their little gathering. "Something I should be aware of?"

Poseidon harrumphed, stomping off toward the large water tank in the far part of the arena. Out of all of them, I knew he was the most pissed that I was involved in academy business. Zeus was his brother, and they'd been… not necessarily close—I didn't think the Gods really did close family relationships—but they had been allies to a certain extent. Poseidon hadn't fought against me and my friends per say, but he hadn't been on our side either.

Hephaistos grunted his usual greeting, then limped over to his large firepit, where he had recruits holding fire and learning how to control it. Demeter sauntered over to her garden, filled with huge trees, vines, and flowers to play with, as well as a bunch of rocks.

Erebus was the only one who came over to talk to me. Well, he actually floated over, as he was perpetually surrounded by misty black shadows. As usual, he was dressed like a Victorian era vampire, resplendent in a top hat sitting jauntily on top his long black hair, frilly shirt, tails, and carrying a black and silver-tipped cane.

"Welcome, Melany," he greeted, his voice like a whisper along my skin.

"Hey, how's it going?"

"It's going well, thank you. Are you ready to do this?"

I shrugged. "I don't think I really have a choice at this point."

"No, probably not."

"Have any tips?"

He grinned, revealing filed down canines. It was like he went out of his way to look the part of the creepy undead. "Yeah, don't kill anyone and you'll be fine."

"Awesome tip. Thanks." I gave him a dirty look, then climbed the stairs to the top platform where the lightning rods were positioned. I'd need them to harness my lightning power so the new recruits could utilize it.

It wasn't long before the doors opened, and the stream of new recruits filed into the building. Demeter greeted them below, splitting them into groups of four to go to each elemental station—fire, earth, water, shadow, and lightning. I was actually nervous as four wide-eyed recruits climbed the stairs to me. I wasn't a teacher; I was a barely functioning person.

My gut started to hurt again. Like someone had

punched me. Frowing, I rubbed a hand over my stomach, wondering which one of the four recruits standing in front of me was the source of my strange reaction. They all looked so unthreatening, so maybe I was mistaken.

I looked at my four pupils, scared to death. Instantly, I recognized two of them from the group in the maze—the eager ginger haired boy, and the willowy brunette with the attitude. To round out my crew, there was a shy, quiet girl with amazing red hair, and another one who looked like she was firmly up the brunette's perky ass.

"So, ah, I'm going to teach you how to handle lightning," I finally managed to stammer, after staring at the recruits for an uncomfortable amount of time.

The brunette rolled her eyes, and right there and then she reminded me so much of Revana that I almost puked.

"Is that how you defeated Zeus? With his own lightning?" the eager boy asked.

I shook my head. "No. I had to use all the elements to defeat him. It was only my combined power that was able to stop him."

"You mean the abilities you stole," the brunette murmured under her breath.

Obviously, she was going to be a big problem.

Stepping forward, I didn't stop until I was only a foot away from her, staring her down. We were around the same height. I was slightly impressed that she didn't back away or lower her gaze.

"I didn't steal anything. The powers were gifted to me by my friends." I glanced over at her hanger-on, who had taken a huge wide berth by now, then back to her. "I'd be careful if I were you, as I'm quite certain you are, like, so close to not having any of those. It would be a shame, as friends are really all that matter in a place like this. It's the thing that will keep you alive."

She swallowed at that, but remained defiant. "Whatever."

"Melany? Everything okay up there?"

Moving away from her, I looked down at Hephaistos, who was glowering up at me—his group of students all gaping along with him.

"Yup." I gave him the thumbs up. "It's all good."

He didn't look convinced, but he went back to his firepit and flames.

I whirled around, startling my group—yes, I sometimes got a kick out of scaring the crap out of people—then went back to stand near the two electrical rods.

"Okay, let's do this." My hands clenched into fists, bringing my lightning power to the surface, until there were white sparks zipping around my fingers and wrists. "Not everyone is going to be able to produce lightning, but you should be able to hold it, even if it is for a few seconds."

"Will it hurt to hold it?" the now-not-so-eager boy asked.

"It can," I answered honestly. There was no point in lying to them. "But you can let go of it any time you want." I nodded to him. "What's your name?"

"Flynn."

"Okay, Flynn. You're up." I set my hand onto one of the rods and released the lightning.

He swallowed, but stepped up next to the rod; his hand shook when he reached for it. I immediately grabbed it, and settled it onto the rod, my palm covering his. He tried to break away, but I held him steady.

"It's okay. It won't kill you. You have the ability to control it inside of you. Trust in that."

As he processed that I felt him start to relax, and I saw the second he noticed the lightning embracing his fingers. His eyes bugged out, but he smiled. I could relate, I had the same feeling when I knew I could control the lightning.

"Oh, my Gods! That's so cool," he gasped.

"Yes, it is." Releasing him, I let him absorb the power.

After he finished, the hanger-on stepped up to the plate. Her name was Amber. I set her hand on the rod. She didn't last as long as Flynn had, but I could tell she realized it wasn't as horrible as she thought it was going to be. Next, was *miss snarky pants,* whose name was Siobhan.

When I reached for her, she pulled away from me. "I can do it on my own, thanks."

"Great. Have at it." I gestured to the rod.

She bit her lip, mustering up the courage while I watched her, and after a few moments she set her hand on the rod.

"Shit!" she hissed, snatching her hand back.

"Not as easy as it looks, huh?"

Her eyes narrowed at me, likely suspecting that I'd increased the power without even touching it. It was true. I did. I had to get my kicks somewhere. Nothing was any fun anymore.

Last up was the shy girl, who murmured her name was Cassandra. I'd never seen someone so timid in my life. She flinched back when I reached for her. It was so bad that I worried that maybe she'd not had a good childhood.

"It won't hurt you."

She nodded, letting me cover her hand with mine, and set it on the rod. I deliberately toned down the voltage for her. I didn't want to scar the poor girl on the first day. If she was going to get through the academy, that would come later.

Within seconds, her eyelids started to flit, and her eyes rolled back into her head. Her whole body began to shake. I took her hand off the rod and she immediately collapsed to the ground, convulsing.

Shit. Did I just kill this girl?

"A little help!" I called out as I crouched beside her, setting my hand behind her head so it didn't smack into the floor.

A moment later, Hephaistos, Demeter, and Erebus flew up to the platform and landed softly next to us. I didn't know where Poseidon was, but I gave him the benefit of the doubt, assuming he was swimming deep inside the water tank with his recruits and hadn't heard my cry for help.

"Well done, Melany," Erebus shook his head. "You killed someone."

"She's not dead. She's having some kind of seizure."

Demeter settled beside me. "Let me."

As the Earth Goddess placed her hand around Cassandra's head to keep it still, I pulled away. I knew

Demeter possessed some healing abilities. You couldn't be tied to the earth and not mend or restore. That was why Georgina was a good healer. Although I'd taken her ability to manipulate plants and the ground itself, she still had the capacity to heal the sick and fix the injured. We had all learned how to heal with potions and tinctures, crazy concoctions brewed by Dionysus. Even I had some skill, but not like Georgina, and definitely not like Demeter.

After a few more minutes, Cassandra stopped seizing, and Demeter settled her head gently on the floor. She carefully patted the girl's cheek, until her eyelids slowly fluttered open. At first, her eyes rolled around, trying to focus, then they lasered in on me, and I felt really unsettled.

"Wh-what happened?"

"She almost killed you." Siobhan smirked.

"I didn't try to kill her," I sputtered. "If I was trying to kill her, she'd be dead. I don't make mistakes." I glared at the brunette, hoping she heard the underlying threat weaved inside my words.

Demeter helped the shy girl sit up. "Do you remember anything before you ended up on the floor?"

"The last thing I remember was Melany saying it wouldn't hurt. Then it all went black."

"I'm going to take you to the infirmary so Chiron

can do a bit of a check up on you." Demeter pulled Cassandra to her feet.

"Okay," she murmured.

After they left, Siobhan, Flynn, and Amber all stared at me.

I made a face. "What?"

"Can we be dismissed?" Amber asked.

"Yeah, go." I waved them off swiftly.

Hephaistos ended up cancelling all the rest of the training. There were some disappointed groans, but most—after seeing what had happened to Cassandra—seemed relieved to be let off the hook. I didn't blame them. I was relieved too. The thought of going through that with another twelve recruits made me feel queasier than I'd felt before this started.

When everyone was gone, Hephaistos shook his head at me. "I told Prometheus that you weren't ready to teach."

"Hey, that wasn't my fault. I swear. I think there's something wrong with that girl."

Hephaistos just sniffed then walked away from me, until I was standing on the platform by myself. Erebus had gone back to his shadows, and Poseidon just glared at me from the edge of the water tank.

I didn't want to be a stupid professor anyway. It was way too much work with no reward. Unfurling my wings, I glided down, then stomped out of the building. I had other, more important things to do. Like find Death and uncover what was going on with the freaking threads. All this other stuff was just a distraction.

CHAPTER TWELVE

MELANY

Once I walked out and crossed the grounds to get to the main building, I saw a continual wisp of shadows keeping in time with me. As I watched Erebus float in and out of my peripheral vision, it gave me an idea.

I stopped walking. "Do you want to help me with something?"

The shadows stopped moving as well, and Erebus stepped out of the swirling dark fog. "Depends on what it is."

"I need to find Thanatos."

He frowned. "Why in Gods' sake do you want to find him?"

"Because I think there is something going on with time and death that could affect everyone."

His expression darkened as he considered the gravity in my words. "How do you think I can help?"

"According to the Furies, Thanatos isn't in the underworld, so that means he must be somewhere on earth."

"The world is a huge place."

"I know, but you could help me zip through the shadows to anywhere within seconds." I tried to play to his ego, of which he had an abundance. "I can't ask anyone else, you're the only one who would be able to help me pull this off."

A spark of intrigue danced in his eyes with my suggestion. "What do I get out of this?"

"Fun. I mean, when was the last time you had any? Besides that, you have nothing else going on right now since classes were cancelled."

"What's wrong with your shadow traveling skills?"

For a moment, I hesitated in answering but sighed. "Since Hades'… since the battle they're rusty. I don't always get to where I'm going."

He nodded. "Yeah, your ties to him were strong."

"I don't want to talk about it. I just want to know if you can go on this little quest with me or not."

He shrugged. "Sure, why not? I've been meaning to visit this cute, little, vintage clothing shop in Romania for some time now."

"Great, you shop while I look for Death."

He held out his hand to me. After a brief hesitation, I took it, and he pulled me into his shadow cloud. We were instantly plunged into darkness.

"Where to first?" he asked, with a cock of his magnificently sculpted eyebrow.

"I don't know. I guess to Pecunia. That's the last place I saw him."

"All right. Let's go."

The mist surrounding us started to swirl, until we were inside a foggy tornado. When it dissipated, we walked out into sunlight and rows of tombstones. Erebus had taken us to the Pecunia town cemetery. That was not what I'd expected.

"Why did you bring us here?"

"We're looking for Death, makes sense we start in one of his favorite type of places." He tipped his hat. "We could go to the morgue if you like instead?"

"No, this is fine."

As I looked around, I spotted a small group of people gathered halfway across the graveyard. They were all dressed in black. A few heads turned toward us, and I felt horrible. Erebus and I had crashed a funeral.

Noticing them as well, Erebus started walking their way, but I rushed to his side and grabbed his arm. "What are you doing?"

"Thanatos might be among the mourners. In the past, he loved to hang out at funerals. I'm pretty sure his favorite was Julius Caesar's. Even I went to that one."

"We're not going to bother those people."

He shrugged. "Suit yourself."

I scanned the cemetery again, looking for someone in a cloak, or hiding in the shadows. As my gaze swept the immediate area, it landed on a pale, square headstone nearby. A name was carved in the stone and flecked with gold. It read, SOPHIA SIDERIS.

My knees nearly buckled, and I had to reach out and grab onto Erebus before I dropped.

"What's wrong?"

Swallowing, I walked toward the grave on unsteady legs, stopping in front of my adoptive mother's gravestone. The tears came freely. It was a beautiful monument to her, and I was so grateful the Demos' had provided it for her when I couldn't.

I startled when I felt Erebus step up next to me and rubbed at my tears, angry that he'd seen them.

"Your relative?"

"My mother."

"Oh, I'm sorry."

"Thanks." I wiped the last of the teardrops, touched the top of the headstone, then turned. "He's not here. Let's keep looking."

"Okay," he conceded with a wave of his hand, and we were instantly enveloped in shadows.

For the next six or more hours, we jumped from country to country, town to town. We stopped at every cemetery, morgue, and hospital we could find. Any place that dealt with death and the dying.

In London, we popped into a car crash that had just happened. There were two people laying on the road bloody and broken. I thought for sure they were both dead, but after a few minutes, I could see them start to move around. The EMT was definitely as surprised as I was.

Erebus insisted we stop at the vintage shop in Romania, and the owners—an old husband and wife team, I assumed—beamed when we opened the door. The little bell above chimed announcing our arrival. In an excited stream of Romanian greetings, they came at the shadow God and grabbed his hands, shaking them profusely.

Gesturing to me, he answered in their language, and I heard my name. The couple's gaze swept me over, obviously not too impressed, then went back to showering Erebus with attention. While they brought out various clothes for him to look at, I walked through the shop, checking out the different period pieces.

My eyes fell on a dark blue, suit jacket and I halted. It reminded me so much of Hades that it was like a punch in the gut. Had he shopped here?

I couldn't imagine it. I mean, it was hard to think that Gods needed to buy anything. Wouldn't they just have it made for them with a snap of their fingers? Although, when Hades had taken me to Nice, we did go to a tailor, who made me the most beautiful dress and hat. Hades had mentioned something about using the tailor for his own suits.

"I want to go to Nice," I blurted out to Erebus.

His eyebrows came up at that. "Why do you think Thanatos would be there?"

"I don't know, I just want to go."

"Okay. Give me a minute, while I pay for all of this and send it back home."

A few minutes later, after hearty goodbyes from the

shopkeepers, Erebus and I stepped back into the shadows.

When we came out into the public square in Nice, my heart was racing. All the memories from being here with Hades rushed back to me. It was stupid of me to think that Hades would be here, but it didn't stop me from scanning the crowd milling about for a handsome, dark-haired man in a gorgeous, three-piece blue suit.

"I have a feeling it's not Thanatos you're looking for here," Erebus murmured from beside me.

I hated being vulnerable again in front of him. So I lifted my chin and pointed to the food cart to the left of us. "I want a couple of ganses. They're delicious." I walked over to the cart and grabbed a couple of the tasty pastries. Hades had bought me some when we were here before, and it had been the best thing I'd ever eaten.

I shoved them into my mouth, but they kind of tasted like ash on my tongue now. "Let's go. There are still a few more places we could try." Although, I was quite certain we wouldn't find Thanatos anywhere. It had been a dumb plan from the start.

After a quick trip to Canada, and the Artic—Erebus wanted to watch the Northern Lights—we ended up back at the academy in the middle of the night. Everyone was asleep. Well, everyone except

Demeter and Dionysus; I could hear them chatting, and the stench of weed coming from one the gardens reached me.

I thanked Erebus for going on the fruitless quest with me, and made my way across campus, to the tiny closet of a room near Dionysus's office that I'd been sleeping in for the past few months.

All of my friends, even Lucian, had offered me a bed in their respective rooms, but I refused. Besides the fact that I didn't sleep much, when I did rest, it was never peaceful. More often than not I cried out in my sleep. When I woke, I was never sure why, as I couldn't quite grasp the dream, but I didn't want to disturb other people's night. Dionysus didn't mind since he barely ever slept anyway, and he said he couldn't really hear me over the bubbling and gurling of his potion making machine.

I sat on the edge of the mattress on the floor, and pulled off my boots, but didn't bother taking off the rest of my clothes. I'd been going to bed in my clothes more times than not. I lay back on the lumpy surface, such a far cry from the luxurious pillow top mattress I had in the underworld, and tried to calm my mind so I could sleep.

Finding Thanatos felt like it was going to be damn near impossible, but I had to keep trying. If seeing those people in that horrific car crash just suddenly get up and move around was any indication, things in the world were getting weirder. It felt like I needed to find out why.

I closed my eyes, picturing the ocean in my mind, hearing the waves crashing against the shore. Those things had always calmed me, and I slowly started to drift away.

Suddenly, I was in a gray fog. I couldn't see anything around me, below me, or above me. It was like I was in a void. "Look!" a voice commanded, low and hollow while echoing around me, but I couldn't tell if it was male or female. "See!"

I was about to shout, "See what?" when a soft yellow glow blossomed in front of me. It grew brighter and brighter, until I could plainly see a cavern lit up by several torches along the rock walls, and white candles positioned on every flat surface there was.

Within that warm glow were three women—I could only assume. Cloaked in long, white, gauzy robes that dragged on the stone floor, they stood with white veils over their faces, completely hiding their identities. Each veil was held in place by a crown of twisted, thorny stems. Blood spots tinged the white sheath underneath those crowns.

One of the women leaned over an old, wooden

spinning wheel. The wheel turned, spitting out a thin golden thread, which one of the other women gathered in her hands. She drew the shiny strand out, wrapping it around her hands over and over. Stopping, she held it up, so the last veiled woman could snipped the line with a huge pair of shears.

Behind them, and all around, I noticed the gold threads hanging down from the ceiling. Each one was a different length. Some were short, while others hung all the way to the ground.

They were the Fates, and I was watching them create a life thread.

"Hello?" I called as I moved forward. They didn't react to my voice, nor did they glance up when I stepped into the cavern. They couldn't see me.

Was I dreaming? It had to be, but it felt very vivid.

The three sisters continued to spin and cut their thread, moving around to hang each one in the cavern as they were created.

"Oh, this one… this is a real nice thread," one of the sisters' clucked as she held up a particular long golden line. "This one will do great things. Great things indeed."

Her sister pointed to a far away spot. "Hang it over there, with the other great ones."

The Fate holding it shuffled across the cavern to the

place indicated. Several threads brushed over her head and veiled face as she moved. When she reached the spot, she let the golden fiber go and it floated in the air, lifting up on some unseen wind, until it reached the ceiling and attached to the rock.

"There. Perfect." She clapped her hands, then turned back to her other sisters, but stopped to look down, where a thick cord of gold lay near the hem of her robe. Crouching, she picked it up, and splayed it through her hands. "Too bad about this one. Although his fall was predicted, it still pains me to see it."

The sister spinning the wheel faced her. "It is always painful to cut off such a life. Yet, even Gods cannot hide from you Atropos."

A God? I frowned, taking a step toward the sister who held the cut thread, wondering if there was any way I could tell who it belonged to.

The woman measuring the golden line coming out from the wheel paused, and her head turned toward another part of the cavern. "I hear something."

"You should hide that thread," the spinner urged, startled. "She's coming for it. She wants to bring him back, and will do whatever she can to change his fate."

"She would not dare interrupt us," Atropos challenged. "Not like last time. She learned her lesson."

My frown deepened. Who were they talking about? Who was this *she?*

That time I also heard the noise coming from another part of the cavern.

The three sisters started to panic, gathering as many threads as they could. "We need to leave," Atropos urged.

The spinner gestured to her spinning wheel. "I cannot leave this here. It would be dangerous in another's hand…"

Her voice trailed off as a thick gray mist obscured the scene, but before everything vanished, the spinner turned her head toward me. Lifting her arm, a long bony finger pointed in my direction.

"You do not belong here!!"

Then I was blown backward, as if hit in the gut by a wrecking ball, and landed on my ass on the hardwood floor. Stunned, I sat there for a moment, blinking away the muddiness of my vision. Eventually, I realized I was sitting on the floor of a corridor I didn't recognize, and no longer in the Fates' cave. It was also plainly apparent that I wasn't in my bed either.

Slowly, I got to my feet, rubbing my face. Had that been real? It felt real. My gaze swept the hallway. Where the hell was I? I definitely wasn't still in Dionysus's Hall. I was in a place I'd never been in before, which wasn't totally odd because the academy was huge. It was comprised of classrooms, training arenas, a dining hall, a great hall, an enormous auditorium, new recruit dormitories, and twelve separate special halls belonging to the twelve Gods of the Pantheon.

I walked down the dark corridor, taking in different things, like the twinkling lights that danced on the ceiling and across the walls. The floor was a dark hardwood, and the tapestries on the walls were mostly dark blue and burgundy. It felt like I should know who those colors represented, but it didn't come to me, not until I came to a huge, bejeweled door about twelve feet high. Swiftly, I realized that I was in Hera's Hall.

I had either sleepwalked across the academy, or used the shadows subconsciously despite my troubles with them, but I'd come a long way for some reason. And that dream? Was it telling me something? Did it have anything to do with Hera? Was she the "she" the Fates had been worried about?

"Melany?"

I whipped around and came face to face with the Star Goddess herself. "Hey," I said lamely. "How are you?"

"What are you doing in my hall?"

"Um, not entirely sure."

"Then I suggest you go back to your end of the academy."

The way she said that seemed as if I was living in the "poor man's neighborhood" of the school. Maybe that's how she felt about Dionysus. Demeter too, I suspected. Now that Zeus was gone, Hera thought herself to be the queen of the castle, and I supposed she was considering she'd been Zeus's long-suffering wife.

I tipped my head to her. "I'll do that. Have a good night."

Hera's gaze was on my back the entire time I walked back down the corridor. It bore into me like a laser beam. The long walk back to my room would give me a chance to figure out why I had ended up here in this hall and what, if anything, it had to do with my dream about the Fates. If that had even been a dream. Yet, if not a dream, then what was it?

LUCIAN

The solid punch to my solar plexus sent me sailing ten feet across the training field. I landed flat on my back, forced to gulp in air. I couldn't breathe. so I rolled onto my side hoping that would make it better. It didn't. Thankfully Heracles was only using half his strength during our sessions, or else I would be nursing a few broken ribs right about now.

"What's wrong with you?" Heracles shouted at me. "That should've been an easy block."

He marched over to me as I struggled to get back to my feet, offering me his hand. I took it and he pulled me up none too gentle. "Your concentration is shit."

"Sorry," I was finally able to say after filling my lungs with much needed oxygen. "My mind is on other things."

"You better not be thinking about Melany."

A simple look was my answer.

He shook his head. "That's all you seem to be doing lately."

"Well, she needs—"

"She needs you to back off. Give the girl some space and time to heal."

I didn't like that he was making too much sense. "It's more complicated than that."

He arched an eyebrow. "Is it? I don't think so." He started back to where we'd been training, before the new recruits came for their first hand-to-hand lesson, which I was going to help teach. I kept in stride.

"Believe me, I know women," he assured, "I've seen Melany's body language around you, and it is screaming *back the hell off*."

I didn't doubt that Heracles knew women. There was an abundance of rumors going around the academy about his prowess with the opposite sex. One count I heard was that he'd had no less than a hundred girlfriends. That sounded like a lot, but considering he'd been around for a millennium, or two, that really was only like one girlfriend per year.

"She's hurting, Heracles," I pressed, as he handed me the padded focus mitts most boxers used. "I can't stand to see it. I have to do something."

"I get it. You love her, and you want to protect her." He slid on another set of mitts. "But sometimes loving someone is all about letting go."

I knew he was right, but it was still hard to hear. I wasn't sure I had the inner courage to let her go.

"Besides that, Melany is one of the toughest mortals I've ever met." He grinned. "Even tougher than you."

"Oh, believe me, I don't deny that." I raised my gloved hands, ready to spar. "It's just like how Athena is stronger than you." I was teasing, of course. Athena was strong, stronger than me for sure, but I was certain Heracles could lift the world if he needed to.

Heracles made a face. "Smarter, most definitely, especially in war strategy, but not stronger." Heracles lifted his arm and flexed his huge bicep. "Nothing can compare to this. I mean, look at it. It's a work of art."

When he did that, it reminded me of my brother Owen. A vivid image of Owen doing just that amongst the clouds popped into my mind. It was so explosive, it made me dizzy and I dropped my hands, side stepping.

Heracles frowned. "Now what? Did you knock your head when I punched you?"

I shook my head, more to dislodge the distracting image from my mind than anything. "It's nothing. I'm good to go." Showing him I was ready, I raised my hands again.

He eyed me for a moment longer, then lifted his mitts. "All right, show me what you got."

I threw a couple of punches that landed firmly against his mitts. When he began to move them up and down, I had to throw an uppercut then an elbow. He kept repositioning, and doing it faster and faster, forcing me to speed.

We went on like that until sweat dripped down my back and over my face. My arms ached from the effort but it felt good.

"There," he concluded as he took off the gloves. "Feel better?"

I nodded.

"Good. Now, get your mind right. We have a class to attend to."

Just as he said that, the door to the academy opened and a stream of recruits came out, filing in on the field in front of us. I recognized Cassandra in the group. She stood in the back, away from the others, but I caught her gaze and gave her a reassuring smile. Her cheeks flushed a bit, and she dropped her gaze to the ground.

I'd heard she had another seizure in elemental class

—during Melany's training. The rumor was that Melany had somehow induced the seizure. In other, less complimentary versions, it was said that Melany had tried to kill Cassandra. Of course, that was all bullshit, but after the rest of the elemental classes had been cancelled, Melany had up and disappeared again.

You'd think I'd be used to it by now.

Heracles gave me a knowing look, but I shook my head at him, making a face. My heart belonged to Melany. He knew that, so I didn't know why he was busting my balls about some cute, yet strange, new recruit. I still couldn't quite remember everything that had happened when I found her in the west wing corridor. Although, I had a sense it had been something significant. I also kept thinking about my brother Owen, and I hadn't done that in over a year—after having reluctantly accepted the fact that I wasn't going to see him again.

We'd been told our whole lives that after we completed the training at the academy, and successfully went through the trials, we would transcend and go to Olympus. It was a reward we'd all hoped to receive.

That hadn't happened to me and my friends. We'd finished the trails, went to war, and became demigods, but no one mentioned going to Olympus. So, I really didn't know where my brother was. That was just one of the many lies we were told by Zeus when we first arrived at the academy.

"Form a single line!" Heracles bellowed.

A few of the new recruits flinched and I tried not to chuckle. I remembered my first time seeing Heracles and being in his presence. It had been awe-inspiring. In a way, it still was. I was honored to call him a friend now.

"The first thing we are going to learn in this class is stance, how to keep your center of gravity. If you perfect this, you will never be knocked off balance, no matter how you move or what hits you."

He'd said the same thing to my class of recruits. It gave me a feeling of *déjà vu* and I shuddered.

Heracles moved to stand in front of the group and put his left leg forward, toe pointing straight, and his back foot pointing outwards. He bent his legs a little and then put up his hands to his chest, hugging his arms a little into his sides.

"Now, from here, I can perform any kind of maneuver." He did an upper cut, then threw two jabs, and an elbow. Then he spun around on his right foot and did a back kick, coming back to rest in the same position. His movements were so quick, his arms and legs blurred.

I heard the gasps in the line.

"In this stance, nothing can knock me over." After a few more moves, he stopped. "Now, normally, we'd be inside in the training room with a couple of wooden dummies rolling out on wheels from the corners of the room, carrying bo staffs. They would take turns hitting me with those staffs, but since we have our own real live dummy." He gestured to me and laughed, which made everyone else laugh. "We don't need to do that."

My lips twitched at his jesting, but I narrowed my eyes at him instead.

He tossed me one of the bo staffs, and with a flick of my wrist, I spun the weapon around my body as I stood in front of him, swinging it over my head expertly.

"Uh oh, looks like someone is showing off."

More chuckles escaped the new recruits.

"It's okay, Heracles. I won't embarrass you… too much."

Heracles snorted. "Do your worst."

He tucked his arm tightly into his body. I did another spin, then smacked him across the shoulder. The crack of it reverberated across the field, and lifted my arms as the wooden pole snapped in half. Splinters of wood rained down onto the ground, a couple even pinged me in the shins.

Pumping his fist in the air, Heracles grinned. Classic move by him. "Ha! I'm still invincible. Nothing, not even the great Lucian, hero of the Battle of Pecunia, can knock me off balance." He brushed off the small wood chips that clung to his shirt.

He turned to the group. "Now, it's your turn."

I could see the looks of horror on their faces at the prospect of being hit with a bo staff.

I chuckled, remembering when Melany had spoken up during our training class, about the idiocy of being hit with a stick on our first day. She'd interested me from the moment I laid eyes on her, struggling and sputtering in the ocean off of pier six, but I think the moment she spoke up in class was when I'd started falling for her.

Heracles ended up pairing us for the training, and I couldn't have been more thankful. We'd been a formidable team.

Although she frustrated me to no end, my feelings for her ran deep.

"Don't worry," I assured the group, "We're not going to be hitting you with sticks."

"Not yet anyway," Heracles barked with laughter.

"Everyone, get into the stance that Heracles showed you." I walked down the line of recruits, inspecting the position of their legs. I stopped to correct a few, then continued.

"Lucian and I will go down the formations, and try and push you over. Don't let us. Whoever can stay on their feet will win a prize."

That produced some smiles in the group. I had no idea what kind of prize he had in mind, but knowing Heracles, it would be something like one on one training, or some kind of lifetime supply of protein powder to increase your muscle mass.

Heracles started at one end of the line and I at the other. The first recruit, a pretty big guy, I was able to push over easily. His center of gravity was way off. He scowled, not liking how easily he had fallen. I went to the next person, a tall girl, and effortlessly moved her. I helped her back up and told her what she was doing wrong. Then I came to stand in front of Cassandra.

She was so small, slim, and short—petite—that I was afraid to push her over, but as I looked down at her feet and legs, I saw that her stance was solid. When I went to shove her, I might have held back a little, but she barely moved.

I smiled at her. "Good job."

She returned my smile, it was shy, hardly a lift of her lips, but it made me feel good to see it.

After going through the line, only Cassandra had remained standing. She looked proud when Heracles congratulated her.

"That's crap," the stocky guy I'd first shoved grunted. "He didn't even push her."

I went to stand in front of him. "What's your name, recruit?"

"Jack."

"Well, Jack, you just earned yourself fifty push-ups."

He groaned. "That's bullshit."

I took a step forward and got in his face. "Do you want to be sent home?"

"No."

"Then do what I tell you, and shut your mouth."

I could sense Heracles moving in beside me. "Do I need to speak with this maggot?"

Jack's eyes got big and he shook his head, dropping to the ground and starting his push-ups.

Heracles smacked me on the back, then moved back to stand in front of the group. "Now it's time to pair up, and try to push each other over."

Before anyone moved, all heads tilted up, and some eyes got wide. One girl looked like she was going to faint. "Oh, my Gods, it's *her*."

I swirled around to see Melany swooping in from high in the sky. My heart picked up a beat, watching her. She was like a dark bird of prey, majestic and fierce. I didn't think the sight of her would ever not give me a bit of thrill in my gut.

"Room for one more?" she asked as she landed.

Heracles grinned. "Absolutely. You can pair up with Lucian, like old times."

While folding her large black wings into her back, she moved toward me. "Yeah, I remember knocking you down within a minute."

I chuckled. "I remember you cheating and sweeping my leg."

"Semantics." She shrugged.

I was happy to see her, and that she looked and sounded like the old Melany. Maybe wherever she had disappeared to, again, had done her some good. Yet, it did give me pause as well. The last time she looked this alive was when she was training with Hades in the underworld. Is that where she'd gone, back to the underworld?

We took up positions in front of each other. We hadn't sparred in over six months, or more. It was going to be interesting. Before I could make a move, Melany cringed, and doubled over, a hand flew to her stomach.

Worry filtered through my pores at the sight. "What's wrong?"

"That feeling of dread again. It hurts." She winced, and straightening, she turned toward the line of recruits. "I'm pretty sure it's coming from one of them."

CHAPTER FOURTEEN

MELANY

"Are you sure?"

I could hear the incredulousness in Lucian's voice, and I hated that he doubted me.

"I've only felt like this when they're around, so it has to be." Then I remembered that it was really bad around the four recruits I had for lightning class yesterday—Siobhan, Amber, Flynn and Cassandra— and right about now, the little redhead was staring at me with her big, odd-colored green eyes.

Was she the source of my pain? It didn't seem possible; she was so timid and shy.

"Are you two going to spar or what?" Heracles

asked, marching over to see what the problem was. That was when he noticed I was doubled over, clutching my stomach. "What's wrong with you?" He got a horrified look on his face. "It's not your lady time, is it?"

I made a face. "No!" I straightened, the feeling of dread was starting to dissipate. "I'm fine."

Lucian rubbed my back, and was about to ask me if I was okay, but my pointed look stopped him. He clamped his lips together. Good choice. I really didn't want to be coddled right now.

"I can take you to the infirmary," Lucian offered.

I shook my head again. "No. You stay and finish your class. I'm going to go rest. I didn't get much sleep last night."

"Where did you disappear to yesterday?"

"It's a long story. I'll tell you about it later."

Lucian nodded, but I could tell he wanted to press me for answers. I appreciated that he didn't and let me hobble off the training field. I glanced over my shoulder as I left and noticed that Cassandra was still staring after me.

Instead of going to rest, I made my way down to the forge to see Hephaistos. I had a project I wanted to talk to him about, and I'd been meaning to get it started for the past month now, but never seemed to have a moment of peace to do it. Plus, it was the one place I knew no one else would be. They either didn't like being squirreled away underground with heat and fire enveloping them, or they didn't like being around Hephaistos.

He was most definitely a grumpy old man, but I had always enjoyed his company. He was one of the first Gods at the academy that I'd considered an ally. Even when he was a jerk and mean to me. I'd always known where I stood with him.

When I climbed up the stone steps to the highest platform where the main forge was, Hephaistos turned toward me. His eyes flashed at me from behind his blacksmithing mask, away from the roaring flames, and he scowled. "Go away. I'm working."

I grinned, happy to be back on familiar ground. "I missed you too."

He grunted and turned back to his work, forging a new sword. It was going to be a huge broad sword, by the looks of the piece of iron he was heating. I slid in next to him, careful not to get in his way. He had a tendency to throw an elbow when someone was too close to him while he was working, well, even when he wasn't working. He'd nearly knocked Diego on his ass during one of our shield-making classes, back in first year when Diego had been talking instead of listening during class.

I watched as he tempered the metal for the weapon; he was surprisingly gentle with his hands, and worked with an ease that only an extremely skilled craftsman could achieve. Hephaistos was an ugly man, with a broad nose and prominent forehead that always made him look like he was scowling, which I supposed was true. He also had deformed lips, and one eye was lower than the other, but he could make the most beautiful things. He was an artist in metalworking, and I hoped he would help me.

As he took the metal out of the fire and to the anvil to forge, he gave me the side-eye. "What do you want?"

"Can't I just come visit my favorite God?"

His scowl deepened. "No. You always want something when you come here."

I was about to argue with him, but pressed my lips tight together. He was right, and this time was no different—well, it was a little bit different.

"Okay, but it's not for me," I shouted over his hammering.

He set the hammer down, sliding the sword blade into the bucket of water next to the anvil. A long bubbling hiss came from the water as it cooled down the red-hot metal. "I'll give you ten minutes of my time, then you can bugger off. I've got important work to do."

"I want to build a metal arm for Gina."

His eyes narrowed. "Hmm, I didn't expect that. You're not normally unselfish."

That made me happy. I hated being predictable. "Despite her not having her earth power, she still works in the garden, so I think having another hand would make her work so much easier." I also hoped it would bring her out of her depression.

He moved over to his worktable, where he had all his drafting tools like large rolls of paper and charcoal, which he used to sketch his blueprints for things. Grabbing a small roll and unravelling it over the wooden surface, he then picked up his charcoal and started to sketch. His hand moved quickly over the surface, and a few minutes later he had a detailed drawing of a mechanical arm.

"Yes! That's perfect." It looked like something from a science fiction movie, with exposed metal rods that would act like tendons. It also seemed to have a cool black glove that would fit snuggly over Georgina's elbow. "It won't be heavy, will it?"

"We can make it out of titanium, or a magnesium-based alloy. I'm sure I can get my hands on something that would work."

I wasn't much of a hugger, but I had an urge to turn and hug Hephaistos for doing this for me. It helped to put my mind and energy on something else for a bit, while I figured out how to find answers about Thanatos and the other strange things happening. I tamped down the urge and just smiled instead. He'd hate it if I hugged him anyway.

"When can we get started on it? I'd love to have it done in a month, it's her birthday soon."

"I have to acquire the materials, but that won't take me long."

I beamed at him, making him extremely uncomfortable, which just made me beam at him even more. "Thank you, Hephaistos. This means more to me than you can imagine."

He lifted his hand, as if he was going to touch my shoulder, but then he squeezed his hand into a fist, and dropped to the table. It made a thumping sound. "Yes, yes. Fine. Now, will you leave me alone? I'm expecting a messenger any moment."

He shouldn't have said that, because now I was intrigued. "What kind of messenger?"

"Argh, girl. You're giving me a headache." He shook his big head, and turned to limp away from me.

It was a dismissal, but I kind of didn't want to leave. I felt more at home here than anywhere else in the academy. It was because it reminded me a bit of Hades' Hall, with all the darkness and fire—a juxtaposition of elements, just like Hades.

"Can I just hang out here for a bit? I won't get in the way. I can make another shield for the armory."

"Don't you have friends to hang out with?" he barked.

I didn't answer. I did have friends, but it wasn't the same with them anymore. Nothing was the same. I definitely wasn't.

"Just for like an hour. I'll work at a different forge." I pointed to the smaller fire pit on the second level. "I can go over there. You won't even know I'm here."

He opened his mouth to answer, with what I assumed was going to be a very loud NO, but a brash noise coming from the stone ceiling drew our attention. I couldn't quite describe the sound. A bit like scratching, or the dragging of something large and heavy across the rock.

It came again, louder, like fingernails down a chalkboard. I shuddered and turned toward the echo. Squinting, I could make out a large chasm in the roof of the foundry. I hadn't noticed it before, but I didn't normally look up at the cavernous room.

"You should leave," Hephaistos warned as his gaze too fixed to the rocks above us.

I could hear apprehension in his voice, so now I was way too curious to go anywhere.

The scratching/dragging got louder and louder, the echo of it surrounding me until it felt like the sound was in my own ears. A large shadow crept across the forge floor, as something big scuttled out of the break in the stone.

Not much frightened me. I'd faced a three-headed demon dog, a floating skeleton who served as a butler, the Furies, Hades, and even Death itself, but what emerged from the vast crack in the rocks made every hair on my body stand on end, and my guts churn.

At first, I wasn't sure of what I was seeing. A pale angular face, black lips, tiny pointed teeth, and long stringy black hair—not unlike one of the Furies, but that was where the similarities ended. Her shoulders were bare and wide, arms slender but muscular, small, yet noticeable breasts, then everything after no longer belonged to a human being.

Beyond her torso was a large bulbous body—black with orange and red markings, much like tiger stripes— lined with tiny black hairs. Six spindly legs sprouted from there, very much of a spider, barbed with short hairs too.

She scuttled even closer, until she was right above us.

I swallowed down the bile rising in my throat, as she lowered herself on white spider silk stuck to the rocky ceiling. I had to step back a few feet to give her room to settle on the stone floor.

"Welcome, Arachne." Hephaistos bowed his head slightly to the human-spider creature.

She turned her head toward me, and I saw that instead of two beady black eyes, each "eye" was made up of eight orbs, and they were all focused on me with an intensity that made me nauseous.

"Who is this?"

I visibly shuddered at her voice. It warbled, like a tuning fork. It made my skin itchy and I had to suppress an urge to scratch at my face.

"This is Melany," Hephaistos replied, giving me a look.

I inclined my head slightly, like I'd seen him do.

That must've satisfied her, because she thankfully turned back to the forge God. "I have your list." One of her spider legs reached back toward her back end, then came away with a web-wrapped scroll. She grasped it with her human hand, handing it over to Hephaistos.

"Thank you." He gently tore away the silk threads, then unrolled the paper. His scowl deepened, and he glanced up at Arachne. "I don't understand. There are no names on this list."

"This was what was given to me to deliver. I do not ask questions of them." Slowly, she ascended back to the ceiling on the silk thread.

"This doesn't make any sense," Hephaistos insisted.

"It is not my concern. I've done my duty." Once on the cavernous roof, she turned and scuttled back to the chasm, the scraping sounds of her six spider legs setting my teeth on edge. A few seconds later, she disappeared into the hollow.

When she was gone, Hephaistos stomped over to the far part of the room, where several shelves lined the wall. It was where all the shadowboxes he'd created were stacked—lovingly side by side. I followed him, curiosity spurring my strides.

"What's going on," I asked.

He set the scroll down on the workspace, staring down at the blank page. He shook his head, rubbing at the stubble on his wide chin. "I don't understand."

"What is this list?"

"The names of those turning eighteen who are being summoned to the academy." He ran his thick fingers over the paper. "It's what I use to send out the shadowboxes."

I peered down at the scroll, realizing my name had

been on that list at some point. "What does it mean when its blank?"

"It means no new recruits are coming to the academy."

"Is that a bad thing?"

He turned his head to glare at me. "Of course it's a bad thing. We will always need recruits for the academy. It has been this way for two millennia."

"Where does the list come from?"

Rubbing his face, he shook his head again, muttering under his breath. "What does this mean? What am I supposed to do?"

I nudged his arm. "Who makes the list? Maybe you can talk to them."

"You can't just talk to them," he scoffed.

"Why not?"

"No one talks to them. It's unheard of, you silly girl."

"Just because no one has done it, doesn't mean it can't be done."

He pinned me with a hard stare. "You do not understand the significance of this, girl. It alters the entire way of things."

"Maybe it was an error. A mistake."

"The Fates do not make mistakes."

CHAPTER FIFTEEN

MELANY

"The Fates?" I frowned.

"Yes, who else do you think determines the path for every single person in the world?" Hephaistos gave me a scathing glance—like I was an idiot. "Who do you think wrote your name down on this scroll so you got your shadowbox?"

Like everyone in Pecunia, I'd learned about the Fates through picture books and stories told in grade school. They were said to be three sisters, in some stories they were beautiful young women with cascading golden hair, and in others, old crones with wrinkled skin and decayed teeth. Clotho spun the thread of life, Lachesis measured its allotted length, and Atropos cut it off with her shears. Every mortal and God had been allotted a thread of life. Some where short, and other's long.

Growing up, I hated to think that there were these three unknown people somewhere in the world sitting around a soinning wheel, deciding how long I was going to live and how I was going to die. I hadn't put much faith in fate. Not until I got that invitation to the academy inside someone else's shadowbox.

"I never got a shadowbox on my eighteenth birthday."

He waved his big hand at me. "Yes, yes, that box was intercepted, but that's why Hades had me—" He stopped talking, then turned and walked away from me.

I caught up to him, my heart racing in my chest. "What did Hades do?"

He growled. "Go away. I need to think."

"I can help. I know something strange is going on. Both Thanatos and Persephone told me about the threads."

Hephaistos's eyes narrowed. "You've spoken with Death?"

I nodded. "Yes, but I need to find him again. Perse-phone told me he probably knows more about what is going on. He must, if something is going on with the Fates. He'd be connected to them."

He let out a long, exasperated sigh. "Let me handle this. It's too big, too important for you to mess around with."

I gaped at him. "Really? After I saved everyone's ass by destroying Zeus?"

"Melany, just do what you're told for once, and stay out of this."

Ha! Like that's going to happen!

"Sure, whatever you say, Heph." I gave him a little salute, then made my way down the broken stone steps to the main floor of the forge.

"You'll be the death of me, girl," he called from the above platform.

I just waved my hand over my shoulder, and walked out of there, runing up the twisting stone staircase to the first floor of the academy. Thankfully, no one saw me come up, so I didn't have to stand there and waste my time explaining why I was down in the foundry.

Now that I knew there was something going on with the Fates, it was even more imperative that I talked to Thanatos. Fate and death went hand in hand. Something catastrophic was happening, I could feel it all the way to my bones.

Maybe there'd be something in the Great Hall

of Learning about Death, and where he liked to spend his time. My stomach rumbled, and I rubbed a hand over it. Food first, though. I was obviously starving.

As I rounded the corner, I nearly ran into the eager recruit from my lightning class, Flynn. "What are you doing skulking around?" I demanded of him.

"I wasn't skulking," he sputtered. "I was looking for the dining hall and got turned around, I think. This place is huge."

I shook my head at his obvious awe of the place. I supposed I'd felt that way once, when I'd first stepped through the front doors and stood in the grand foyer. Zeus stood on the giant staircase, ominously telling us what we should expect. It was a bit of a culture shock to be sure.

I decided to take pity on Flynn. "Yeah, it can be confusing," I agreed. "All the halls here do look the same."

He smiled. "Right? You'd think that with all this Godly power around, they'd manage to put up a sign with flashing arrows that said *Dining Hall, That Way*."

"Maybe let Dionysus know. He loves flashing lights." I chuckled. "I'm sure he could make a sign for that."

"Are you heading there too? Maybe we could walk

together. I have so many questions I want to ask you. You're like a legend in Pecunia."

"You're from Pecunia?"

He nodded, and was about to say something else, when another voice came from behind us.

"There you are."

I turned to see Lucian striding down the corridor toward us. "Yup, here I am."

Flynn seemed incredibly nervous as Lucian approached.

"Lucian, this is Flynn. He's one of the new recruits, and has an affinity to lightning."

His eyes widened. "I do?"

"Yup, I felt it during class."

Lucian held out his hand toward him. "Good to meet you, Flynn."

"You too," he replied, looking about nervously. "I'll be going. See you later." He quickly walked away, down the hall toward the dining hall.

"What was that all about?" Lucian asked.

I shrugged. "Nothing. He got lost or something."

"I think he has a bit of a crush on you."

I gave him a snide look. "Not likely."

"Oh, I think so. I recognize that puppy-eyed look anywhere. It's the same way I look at you." Laughter escaped him as he wrapped his arms around me.

I squirmed a little in his arms but I didn't pull away. Then he kissed me and I stopped moving altogether. I leaned into him, finding familiar comfort. Something I'd been missing for a while.

When Lucian pulled back, he searched my face. He did that a lot lately. He likely knew I was keeping so much from him. "Where did you run off to? The forge?"

He also knew me pretty well.

I nodded. "Yeah, there was something I needed to talk to Hephaistos about. Then the craziest thing happened."

"What?"

I told him about meeting Arachne, and the shadowbox list with no names on it.

"What does it mean?"

"I'm not sure, but it obviously has something to do with the Fates." I thought about my dream. Maybe it wasn't really one, and it had been something else. A portent? A vision of the future, or of the past?

"I also had a strange dream," I admitted.

His face darkened. "About what?"

"I was in a cave, somewhere, I'm not sure where, and there were three veiled women spinning golden thread…"

"The Fates?"

I nodded. "Yes, I'm pretty sure. They were talking about someone trying to fix a thread or reweave it, I don't know which."

"Who?"

"I don't know, but they mentioned 'she.'"

He scratched his chin. "Could be anyone."

"True, but the thread they were talking about belonged to a God, I am sure of that."

"Zeus'?"

I shrugged. "Quite possibly." That had been my first thought, but I also didn't tell him that my next thought had been of Hades. "So, maybe the 'she' in this equation belongs to Aphrodite."

He made a face. "I don't know, Mel. There are a lot of 'shes' who might want to see Zeus again. Hera for one. She is his wife. Artemis was pretty close to him as well. Besides that, Aphrodite's locked away in Tartarus…"

"Yes, but she would be the one who would benefit the most from Zeus's resurrection."

"There's no way she can escape Tartarus. Prometheus has the key."

"Well, they were scared of someone. I heard noises in the cave, like someone was there. They looked startled, like they were going to run or something. Then I was literally knocked out of the vision."

"What do you think it means?"

"I don't know. But something is going on with Fate, and time and death."

His expression changed again, and he swallowed at the dire implication.

"What?" I asked him. "You know something."

"I don't know if I know anything, but I had an odd dream the other night as well."

"About?"

"My brother, Owen."

That surprised me. Lucian had only mentioned his brother once or twice since I knew him. "What happened in the dream?"

"I'm not entirely sure. I was in Olympus, and he was there. He mentioned something about time being broken, that I needed to fix it. Then I was being pushed out of there, and his last words were 'she will help you'."

That was definitely interesting and I was sure had something to do with what I'd dreamt. "Who do you think this 'she' is?"

"I have no idea."

I wondered if the "she" in his dream had any connection to the "she" in mine. It was possible.

"I want to find out more about the Fates and where this cave is."

"We could check in the Great Hall of Learning. That's where we found out the truth about the academy."

"You want to help me?"

He smiled at me. "Of course. You don't even have to ask. Besides, this way I can keep that love-sick Flynn away from you."

I gave him a side-eye. "You're not jealous, are you?"

He scoffed. "Of course not."

Yet, I thought maybe he was, just a little. "Right." I laughed.

He gave me one of his knowing lopsided smiles that always produced little flutters in my belly. Today, was no different. I had to be honest, I was grateful, and relieved for that response.

Swinging his arm around my shoulders, we walked together to the main stairwell that would take us to the Great Hall of Learning. A month ago, even a few days ago, I might've pushed his arm off, claiming I had something else to do. I was happy that I didn't feel the urge to do that this time.

Maybe things could get back to normal.

Lucian definitely noticed, and it was clear it pleased him. "Feels like old times," he admitted, as though reading my thoughts.

"Yeah, a bit."

"I'm glad. I guess it just took another dangerous mission for you to feel more like yourself."

At that I made a face. "That's not true."

"Mel, you are a danger junkie. You might as well admit it."

"Fine," I sighed. "But then, what does that make you?"

"A Blue junkie."

I laughed, feeling good for the first time in months. I didn't know if it was the fact that we were on a mission, trying to solve a new mystery, or if it was being with Lucian in a relaxed manner. Maybe it was both. I'd like to think that was true. Despite all my pushing him away and serious emo attitude for the past few months, I'd missed him. I'd forgotten how he made me feel.

I vowed to myself I'd do better by him. That I wouldn't treat him as disposable, or unwanted anymore. To be honest, he deserved better than me. I'd told him that once, and I remember he'd nearly yelled at me because of it. He did call me stupid though. No matter how shitty I was to him, Lucian stayed by my side, and I didn't know what I did to be worthy of him. Nothing I could grasp now.

"What are you thinking about?" he asked.

"Nothing. Why?"

"Because your nose is all scrunched up. It's cute as hell, but I know it means you're thinking pretty hard about something."

"Just trying to fit all the pieces together."

"We'll figure it out."

"Yeah, I know."

"Then quit worrying." He leaned down and pressed his lips to the side of my head.

I nodded, but I wasn't convinced this was going to be easy. Nothing since coming to the academy had been easy for me. It was one mountain after another to climb, but I supposed that was got me excited about it all. The challenge.

As we entered the library, I was most definitely thrumming with energy. I had to admit it—although I would never do so out loud to anyone, not even Lucian—that I was pumped at the prospect of going up against Aphrodite again. I was almost certain she had a hand in all of this. She wasn't the type of Goddess to be a gracious loser.

She'd vowed to me before she'd been carted away to Tartarus that she would get her revenge on me somehow. Maybe this was the start of it.

I smiled to myself.

I really hoped so...

Bring it on, bitch!

CHAPTER SIXTEEN

MELANY

*L*ucian and I didn't find much useful information about the Fates in the library. Really not that much more than I'd learned from picture books as a kid. Definitely nothing that pointed me toward where I could find them anyway.

We just read about each of the sisters and what their duty was. Supposedly, they also determined how someone died and what their fate was during their life-time. They did that for both mortal and gods alike. So, they were really the most powerful and important enti-ties to exist.

They decided who lived or died.

Though, I couldn't find in any texts whether a life thread could be altered after it had been cut. I supposed the Fates wouldn't want that kind of information readily available, or else everyone would try to find them to bring back their loved ones.

Believe me, it was at the forefront of my mind.

After spending a couple hours in the library, Lucian convinced me to come to the dining hall for dinner. We sat at our usual table with Jasmine and Mia—I was happy to see their relationship was still going strong—Georgina, Ren, Diego and a few others. At first, it was a bit awkward, but it didn't take long before we were all talking and laughing, like the past few months hadn't happened and altered all of our lives.

Jasmine gave me a hard time when an eager new recruit—a tall, gangly girl with long black hair, and huge muddy brown eyes—approached our table to ask me for an autograph. She wanted me to sign the t-shirt she had on under her academy uniform. I was so shocked by the request that I signed her shirt without a word. Although, I did draw the line when she asked if she could hug me.

Jasmine threw a French fry at me after the girl had left, and rejoined her new recruit friends. "You have a fan. How does it feel to be an uber celebrity?"

"Stupid to be honest."

Hella shrugged. "I don't know, I think you earned it. You kind of did save us all."

I didn't know what to say to that, so I just shoved a piece of pepperoni pizza into my mouth instead.

Knowing I'd rather change the subject, Lucian told everyone about Flynn being all gaga for me, prompting another round of good-natured ribbing. I told them to shut up, and scanned the cafeteria for the boy in question, but couldn't spot him. Maybe he'd already eaten and had returned to his dorm.

I did lock eyes with Cassandra though. She was sitting pretty much by herself at one of the far tables while staring at us—at me. It was so unnerving that my stomach started to ache again. The feeling of dread had to be coming from her, but I had no idea why. I wanted to drill her about it, but I didn't think anyone would be on my side about interrogating the poor timid thing.

After dinner, Lucian wanted to go flying to the lake, but I opted to spend some time with Jasmine and Georgina, as I felt like I needed my girlfriends more. We hadn't done much together since the battle.

They planned a girls' night in Georgina's room, which was in in Demeter's Hall. The plan was to watch something girly and romantic, eat junk food, and Mia really wanted to paint everyone's nails. I hadn't painted my nails in over a year, longer even. It seemed like an indulgence, but maybe that was what we all needed.

There was five of us crammed in Georgina's room. Me, Georgina, Jasmine, Mia, and Hella who had been Jasmine's old roommate back in first year. She seemed nice; I'd never had an issue with her, but neither did I know her all that well, despite the fact that we'd gone into battle together twice. She was a good fighter, excellent with a spear, that was all I really knew about her. I supposed this would give me a chance to get to know her as well as reconnect with Georgina, Jasmine and Mia.

I sat cross legged on the floor as bags of sour cream and onion chips, and Cheetos were handed around the room. I grabbed a handful of cheesy goodness. "Where did you get the junk food?" Usually the food at the academy was all about health and getting strong. I was pretty sure Heracles had a hand in devising the menu.

"I asked Dionysus if he could score us some contraband." Georgina grinned, orange Chceto dust flecking her lips.

I laughed, delighted with her. In the past, she'd been one to stick to the rules. She wasn't a fanatic about it, but we'd had our fair share of arguments over them. Especially, during those first few months in first year. Despite that though, she'd been a great room-mate, and an even better friend.

It made me glad that she hung out with Dionysus once in a while. Although he was a bit on the insane side, he was also trustworthy. I knew he'd never hurt Georgina. He was just about having a good time for a long time.

Looking at Georgina, thinking about our past friendship, I almost felt teary. So, I shoved the orange sticks in my mouth to stop the flow of emotion threatening to overwhelm me. I had a feeling she spotted it anyway, because she came over to sit beside me on the floor.

She nudged me with her shoulder. "I've missed you, Mel."

"I haven't gone anywhere. Well maybe the other day and night when I kind of disappeared…"

"That's not what I mean, and you know it."

My expression softened. "I know. And I'm sorry I've been so in my head."

She grabbed my hand. "Tell me what's going on. I might not be able to help, but I can listen. I can try to understand."

I squeezed her hand. I'd been so angry and sad after the battle, in pain, trying to deal with all these powers inside of me, I hadn't just sat down and talked it out with anyone. I thought my friends had been scared to ask me how I was doing. Lucian had asked, almost every day, but I knew I couldn't tell him how I was really feeling. He wouldn't understand. Especially, when I wanted —no needed—to talk about Hades without judgement.

Georgina was offering that to me.

"I'm sad, Gina." I drew my hand through my hair, knowing it likely stuck up all over the place, and sighed. "I'm also angry. Devasted. Frustrated. I've never been so full of emotion before. It's hard to know what to feel and when."

"You've been through serious trauma. We all have." She shrugged her shoulder, bringing attention to her missing arm. "I mean, we fought in a war, Mel. We saw people die. You more than most."

I knew she wasn't just talking about Hades, but about Revana. I'd been the last person to talk to her before she fell into the deep chasm in the earth. I sometimes still dreamed about that moment, when I tried to reach her, tried to keep her from falling. I'd wake up in a cold sweat, fresh tears on my cheeks.

Revana and I had never been friends. She was an awful person and consistently tried to hurt me, but she still didn't deserve to die like that. I knew it wasn't my fault, but a ball of guilt still got stuck in my throat every time I thought about her.

"I miss him."

I didn't have to clarify, she knew I was talking about *him*. Everyone did.

It still hurt when some people whispered about him behind their hands, like he was somehow a dirty little secret. I wanted to shout at them. Hades may have had a questionable past and reputation, but he had risked his life for us. For me. He was more heroic than I'd ever be.

"I know that no one understands why. Everyone thinks we had some strange, forbidden relationship, but I loved him. I truly did."

Her nose crinkled a little, but she didn't say anything. She didn't like him, juast as everyone else. Georgina didn't understand how I could love a God who had essentially kidnapped me, and forced me to train with him and the Furies. But she didn't see him like I did. She didn't get a chance to uncover the raw emotions inside him. Everyone thought he was evil, devoid of compassion and sympathy, but Hades had a huge heart. It was just darker than most.

Sighing, I rested my head back against the wall. "I know you don't get it. You didn't know him like I did."

She nodded. "I know. And whether I get it or not, I

can see the pain you're in." She put her good arm around me, and pulled me into her.

Georgina was a natural born healer. Even without her earth powers, I could feel the compassion and empathy she harbored seeping into me. A warmth spread over my skin, reminding me of the hugs I used to get from Sophia. I leaned my head against Georgina's shoulder and let her take some of my pain away with her friendship.

As we sat there together, my gaze caught Jasmine's from across the room. She gave me a soft smile, and I returned it. Our friendship was not as easy as mine and Georgina's. I loved her, but she'd challenged me in the past, especially about my relationship with Hades. She hadn't been a fan of his at all. We'd argued on several occasions, fought even, but I'd always known in the end that she had my back, and that I had hers.

The chips were eaten while Hella talked about her crush on Diego. She was trying to get up the nerve to tell him that she liked him, but worried that he wouldn't like her back. I chuckled at the very girly discussion we were having. It was so out of place in an academy for demigods and soldiers.

"Hella, you are a spear maiden and kickass soldier in the Gods' Army, if he doesn't fall at your feet, he's a friggin' idiot," I declared, grabbing the near empty bag of Cheetos, and shoved some into my mouth.

That made everyone hoot and holler in agreement.

"Yeah!" Jasmine shouted as she high fived Hella.

Mia crawled over to where Georgina and I were sitting, extending a hand toward me. "Give me your hand. I want to paint your nails."

I slapped my hand in hers, and she took out a bottle of shiny gold nail polish. She unscrewed the lid, took out the brush and painted on the color on my thumb-nail. The color sparkled in the light. It was very pretty. Not my usual style, but Mia seemed to love it, so I didn't argue.

"Where did you get nail polish?"

A wicked gleam entered her eyes, and she grinned. "I totally raided Aphrodite's rooms before they were turned into the Hall of Heroes."

I shook my head, but chuckled. "You're lucky you didn't get caught." Also, I kind of wished I'd had a chance to join her. I would've love to have stolen some of the Goddess'possessions out of spite.

"Ha! What are they going to do to me at this point? We've already been to hell and back."

I laughed. She was right. What were they going to do at this point? We'd all passed the extremely difficult trials. All of us became soldiers in the Gods' Army, and we'd been in a huge battle with Gods and monsters. Taking away privileges, or confining us to our rooms, weren't really punishments anymore. I imagined some of us would gladly stay in our rooms for an undetermined amount of time. To rest. To sleep. To not have to think about all the shit we'd just been through and done.

While Mia continued to paint my nails a flashy gold color, I thought about Aphrodite. Was she trying to find a way to resurrect Zeus? Or was I just projecting my own desires for a resurrection onto her? The Fates had been talking about someone. A female someone. Someone they seemed a little bit, I wouldn't say scared, more like concerned. I didn't think the Fates feared anyone. Why would they? They had all the power.

Yet, they had been nervous. I didn't blame them. The thought of someone resurrecting Zeus scared the crap out of me, because I knew he would be impossible to beat again. I'd had one chance to overcome him, using every bit of power that resided inside me. I wouldn't be able to achieve that again.

If Zeus returned to power, everyone in the entire world would be in danger.

For the past few months, with Chiron's help, I'd been trying to remove the powers I'd received from my friends, but it wasn't working. What I didn't tell the centaur was I suspected that the energy inside me wasn't going to leave no matter what we did. It had fused into my muscles and bones, and I could feel it weaving its way deep into my soul. Eventually, the power would take over, and when it did, I feared I'd explode taking anyone within a very large radius with me.

So really, in some weird way, Zeus would still get his revenge on us all.

CHAPTER SEVENTEEN

MELANY

After painting our nails, eating all the junk, and watching a really funny movie about a couple of nerdy girls graduating high school, I said my good-byes and made my way across the academy to Diony-sus's Hall, and into my room.

I took in the small mattress on the floor, a wardrobe to put my clothes in, of which I didn't have many—just a few T-shirts, my leather pants, joggers, and my armored one piece that Hades had designed for me to use in battle—and sighed. I'd left the rest of my stuff back in my room in Hades' Hall. All the sexy dresses and get ups Hades had enjoyed seeing me in. Gods, how I ached to be back in that room, in that hall, with him.

I pulled off my boots and laid down on the mattress, shoving the pillow under my head, and thought about all those outfits Hades would lay out for me in the morning. The first time he did it, I refused to wear what he'd set out, opting for my usual ripped jeans and T-shirt. The next time, he vanished all my clothes so I had to wear what he wanted, and I remembered being so mad at him for that little trick of his.

My gaze swept the small room, and landed on the only other thing I'd managed to get out of the hall—a painting of the moon and stars reflected in a quiet pool of water. A street artist had used spray paint and various metal objects to create the art piece. Hades bought it for me for an obscene amount of money, when he'd unexpectedly taken me to the Battle of the Flowers carnival in Nice. It had probably paid for that artist's rent for a whole year.

As I stared at it, I felt myself start to drift, not realizing how tired I truly was. My eyelids fluttered shut, and I suddenly fell into a dream world…

I was back in Nice, in the town square near the harbor, while the top of the Ferris wheel rose over the old stone buildings that surrounded the square. There were masses of colorful flowers strewn over the cobblestones, like there had been that day, after the carnival floats passed through it. I remembered thinking it was like walking on rainbows. I smiled now at the thought.

Unlike that day, where the square was packed with musicians, dancers, and street artists, as well as carnival goers in colorful costumes and masks and pretty hats, I was alone in the street. Music came from somewhere though.

As I moved across the square, I was acutely aware that I was wearing the same dark blue and black dress that I'd worn that day. I was also wearing the big hat with feathers and lace, and the black mask coverd my face.

When I neared the food cart that sold ganses, the smell of the deep-fried pastry filled my nose, and my stomach rumbled in response. I remembered eating one that day for the first time and falling in love with the taste. It had been pure happiness on my tongue. No one manned the cart, but a couple of pastries sat on the counter, still warm and fresh. I couldn't resist, and I picked one up and ate it.

"You love those things, don't you?"

I whirled around at the voice, but there was no one there. His voice had been right in my ear and I swore I could feel his presence behind me. I searched for the square for him, and saw movement near the corner of the building.

I ran towards the stone structure, a souvenir shop, and turned the corner, certain I was going to see Hades standing there. Except, the lane was empty. Movement to the right had me running in that direction too, but when I rounded the corner again, the street was empty, although bright flower petals fluttered over the cobblestones.

"Hades!" I shouted. My voice echoed off the buildings, bouncing back to me.

This was my dream, wasn't it? Surely I could conjure him with a thought.

I squeezed my eyes shut, and pictured his face in my mind. After counting to three under my breath, I then opened my eyes. I whirled around in a circle. I was still alone.

"Hades!" I shouted again. "I know you're here somewhere. Quit playing games. I am so not in the mood."

"What are you in the mood for then?"

Spinning around, I saw him leaning up against the wall of the building behind me, looking cavalier, and extremely sexy. He wore the dark blue suit jacket with the high collar he had on that day, as well as the frilly white shirt and dark tight pants. His grin blossomed under the lacy, black half mask on his spectacular face.

My knees nearly buckled at the sight of him.

As quick as I could, I strode toward him, afraid he was going to disappear before I reached him, but he didn't. When I wrapped my arms around him, I closed my eyes, and sighed with relief. He was back in my arms. I could finally breathe again.

"Are you happy to see me or something?" he teased.

"Shut up and kiss me."

"As you wish. It is your dream."

I pulled back to look him in the eyes. "Is it? Is it really a dream?"

"Of course it is, Melany." He smirked. "You saw me die right in front of you."

I searched his face, looking for a sign that he was putting me on, that he'd tricked me and everyone else into believing that he died. Yet, he didn't give anything away.

Hades met my gaze full on, there wasn't any deception in his eyes or the way he looked at me. I looked hard for it, for anything, clinging to the hope that somehow his death hadn't been real. I knew I was deluding myself.

Sorrow and heartbreak filled me. It was almost like

losing him all over again, but I wouldn't let this dream go to waste. It was the first time he'd ever come to me.

Several times over the past few months I would dream of searching for him, but I was never able to find him. Now, I could touch him, kiss him, be with him. I knew it wasn't real, that I'd never have that again, but for a moment, while I slept, I could pretend it was authentic. That he was alive and in my arms.

I buried my fingers into the silk of his dark hair and kissed him. He wrapped his arms around my waist, flipping me around, until I was pressed against the stone wall. Before deepening the kiss, he made a small sound low in his throat then dipped his tongue into my mouth and nipped on my bottom lip with his teeth. I let out a long, satisfied moan, eager for more.

Oh, Gods. I was on fire for him. A jolt of energy tingled through my body, until white sparks actually erupted from my skin. They jumped over to him, sizzling over his face and down his neck.

Hades pulled back, gifting me with that wry sexy grin of his. "Well, this is new."

Slightly embarrassed by my unbridled reaction to him, I dipped my head, avoiding his gaze.

Hades put his finger under my chin, and lifted it so our eyes met. "You never have to be embarrassed with me. I like it. You're powerful, Melany. Revel in it. Use it to your heart's content."

His words filled me with vigor. I loved that he wanted to celebrate my darkness. He'd always encouraged me to let go of the constraints I put on myself to stop from being so different, so extra, around my friends. Even before I'd siphoned their individual elemental energy to end Zeus, I'd been more powerful than any of them. I tried not to be, tried to rein it in but it was difficult, and tiring.

It was especially that way with Lucian. It was one of the reasons I hadn't wanted to have sex with him. We'd attempted to a couple of nights, but each time I felt like I had to hold back. I couldn't completely let myself go with him. I was afraid of hurting him, and the last thing I wanted to do was hurt him.

I loved him.

Maybe not in the way I loved Hades, but my heart was still full of affection, attraction, and the desire to see him happy.

I just didn't think I was the one meant to make him happy.

I pressed my lips to Hades' mouth, nibbling on it, then down to his neck letting my teeth sink. He let out a long sexy groan, his hands reaching down to mold my ass.

"I've missed you," I murmured against his ear, then trailed my tongue over the lobe.

"I can tell." He groaned again, deep in his throat, as my hand wandered down the front of his shirt, pulling a button open and feathering my fingers over the hard, smooth plane of his chest.

"Did you miss me?" I couldn't keep the pleading out of my voice, but I tried not to be embarrassed by it.

"I'm dead, darling. I don't have any emotions."

I pulled back and looked him in the eyes again. "I don't believe you. I don't believe you're dead."

He stroked his fingers over my cheek, the pad of his thumb caressed my lips, and he clucked his tongue. "You have to stop this foolish notion. No matter how many times you wish it, there is no weaving me back to life. It's time to cut the ties and move on."

"I don't want to."

"I know." He leaned in and brushed his lips against mine.

I sighed, holding back the tears that threatened to fall. "Can I have this one last night with you then?"

He smiled, his dark eyes glinting with passion. "Of course. It's your dream. You can have whatever you want."

"Then I want you to take me. Here, now."

Hades didn't hesitate to fulfill my demands.

With one powerful rip, he tore my dress off, until I was standing there in just a pair of thigh-high fishnet stockings, my big hat and lacy mask. At one time I would've been embarrassed by the way my nipples instantly hardened, and by the goose flesh that pebbled every inch of my skin, but now, here with Hades in my dream world, I was brazen with desire.

My whole body lit up. Sparks sizzled along my breasts and belly, down my legs. Flames erupted from my fingertips, and slowly crawled up my arms. I could hear the waves crashing against the harbor not far from us. The scent of the ocean air surrounded us in a mist. The stones that my back pressed into seemed to soften, holding me close, like a lover's hand.

All my power leapt to life, and at the very heart of it, wrapping around my body, caressing every part of my flesh, kissing me, were the shadows of darkness. Hades embodied everything about that element.

His one hand cupped the back of my leg, and yanked it high, entering me in one quick thrust that set off the explosive energy inside of me.

"Hades!" I cried out his name as he made love to me...

I sat up in bed, sweat drenching my clothes. My heart pounded against my ribs making it painful to breathe. My hands shook as I rubbed my chest and tried to regulate my breathing. Every muscle in my body quivered, especially the ones between my thighs. Desire, thick and heady, still throbbed deep inside.

It was dark in my room, but I sensed movement in the corner near the door. Peering into the shadows, I swore I saw a face, but as quickly as it appeared, it was gone. I rubbed a hand over my mouth, and flopped back onto the mattress.

I'd had vivid dreams before, but this one took first place. I could still feel his hands on my skin, and his lips on mine. I raised my hand to rub at my eye, and my fingers brushed across a strip of lace. Sitting up again, I tugged off the mask that had been tied around my eyes and stared down at it in my hand. Shock and hope swirled around in my belly.

Seconds later, the lace dissolved in my fingers, until there was nothing left but a whisper and a promise.

CHAPTER EIGHTEEN

MELANY

The next day, I was dragging my ass around the academy. I was so tired. After my extremely vivid sex dream about Hades, I didn't really go back to sleep. I drifted in and out for another few hours, until I finally got up at around five in the morning.

Thankfully, there weren't too many people around, just a few of the Gods, like Heracles, who was working out, and Dionysus, who was day drinking. I suspected he never slept anyway, so I was able to get in some physical training before the new recruits were up and about.

I really didn't want to be gawked at, or fawned over, and I most definitely didn't want a bunch of groupies asking for autographs. It was times like these that I was grateful for the no cellphone policy at the academy, or else I'd be dodging fans wanting to take selfies with me to post on their Instagram accounts.

I so didn't want to be Insta-famous.

After I ran twenty laps around the outdoor training field, which amounted to about five miles, I did a hundred push-ups, sit-ups, and the worst thing ever—a hundred burpees. Even Gods and demigods hated those evil things.

Once I was finished with the last one, a shadow fell over me while I was on the ground. I looked up to find Medusa looming over me, a sword in each hand, green tendrils of hair swirling around her head. Only after months of sparring with her, had I finally realized that her hair was actually a bunch of tiny snakes, with tiny black beady eyes.

I couldn't tell if she was glaring or not as she wore her dark sunglasses to cover her white, stone-inducing eyes, but I suspected she was.

"Can I help you, Medusa?" I asked as I got back to my feet. Fifteen months ago, seeing her would've had me shaking in my boots, but now not so much. She was definitely formidable, imposing, and scary looking, but we both knew that now I had more power than she did.

"Looking for a sparring partner. You up for it?"

"Sure. I've got nothing better to do today."

She tossed me one of the swords, then assumed a fighting stance—her blade raised, and poised to strike. I took a couple steps back, also lifting my sword. She had a good five inches on me, so taking that into account, I had to change the way I defended as most of her attacks would likely come from an overhead swing.

I had only seconds to prepare before she swung at me, and I'd assumed right, it came from above me. I deflected her steel, faded to the back, then advanced. She blocked it, performing a similar move, until we were crossing the field back and forth, trading volleys with our swords. The clash of metal echoed through the air, and I imagined could be heard from miles away with the amount of force we were both using in our attacks.

It wasn't long before my arms were aching from the strength, and exertion of lifting and swinging five pounds of steel and iron, but I had a grin on my face. This was exactly what I needed right now. A big old distraction. A chance to use my skills.

There was nothing better to cheer a girl up, than by trying to strike a six-foot-tall demigoddess with snakes for hair and a snarky attitude. I could see, she too, was having a good time trying to slice me open with the edge of her blade. It was a win-win.

By the time we both began showing some fatigue, we'd gained a varied audience. Several of the new recruits, and most of my peers, lined the training field cheering us on. A few of the Gods and demigods, also stood around us. Most seemed to be cheering for me, but there were a few Medusa fans, which included Achilles, Helen, and Antiope—they had all fought with Medusa in the final trial, mock battle during my first year.

I risked a look over to the sidelines when I heard my name. Lucian and Jasmine stood next to each other, calling out to me. I also was hit with that painful sensation of dread in my gut and I winced. That brief distraction was enough for Medusa to take advantage. She thrust her sword at me, feinted to the right, then came around with a spinning attack. The edge of her blade ran across my shoulder blade and cut open my shirt as well as my skin. The sting was immediate, and I hissed in pain.

The crowd watching also reacted, with a couple of cheers by Achilles and company, and more than a few boos from those who supported me. Yet, I didn't let the injury slow me down. Out of the corner of my eye, I noticed Medusa celebrating her victory in cutting me by lowering her sword and grinning at her friends. Big mistake.

I took a step back with my left foot, pivoted, swung my sword around and up just as she was turning back toward me. My steel sliced right by her head. I imagined she would've felt the puff of air against her face as my blade passed by, and then heard the hisses of the snakes as I cut right through them. Little green heads landed on the ground.

Medusa shrieked, reaching for her hair that fell flat against her head. "You bitch! I'm going to kill you for that!"

Just as she reached for her sunglasses, intending to turn me into stone with her freaky eyes, my hand came up, lightning flashing along my fingers and around my arm. I could shoot a hole through her, before she was even able to use her power on me. Thankfully it wasn't just a matter of her looking at me, she had to generate that power to turn people to stone and decide to use it. I suspected she wouldn't hesitate to use it on me.

"Don't," I warned. "I don't want to kill you."

She shrieked again. I could hear the frustration in those high-pitched decibels.

"Your hair will grow back, just as the cut across my back will heal," I pointed out, since our injuries were two-sided. We both knew the little snakes on her head would grow back within days. I would never have done that, if that hadn't been the case. Medusa and I weren't friends, but I didn't want to hurt her in a way she'd never recover from either. Although I suspected, she wouldn't have afforded me the same courtesy, and if she could've injured me more, she would have.

Lucian, Jasmine, Helen, and Achilles all ran out onto the field, probably to try and stop a possible blood bath. Or, with the way Helen glared at me, encourage one.

Obviously, she was still mad, as she reached for her glasses again.

"Keep your glasses on, Medusa," Achilles urged.

"We're all on the same team," Lucian reminded as Medusa continued to screech and accuse me of trying to kill her without provocation.

"Ha! Don't be so naïve kid," she growled, "We will never be on the same team," she assured, but she didn't attempt to remove her sunglasses again. So that was progress at least.

Closing my hand, I killed the lightning inside it. Honesty, I'd always admired her. It made it easy to know who were your friends, and who were your enemies. I hated this machiavellian politeness that had settled over the academy since I took down Zeus. I knew a few of the Gods and demigods would take me out if they could in retaliation. Aphrodite had more allies than just Ares, I was sure.

Before anything else could happen, a scream echoed across the training field. We all whirled around to see a group of the new recruits, and my peers, circling a body on the ground. Lucian ran toward the crowd, and I followed closely—Medusa's sword still clutched in my hand. Jasmine was right beside me.

The circle opened up for us, to show that it was Cassandra who had collapsed; she was having another seizure.

"Move back!" Lucian shouted to the others, crouching next to her to support her head. "Give her some room."

I, along with everyone else, took a few steps back. As I moved, I noticed Siobhan and Amber standing next to me. The evil sensation in my gut amplified, and I nearly doubled over from the pain.

Siobhan sneered at me. "It's your fault. You damaged her."

I was about to respond to her bullshit accusation when something, or someone, punched me in the side of the head. I saw black spots in my vision and I dropped to my knees. There were several gasps from people around me.

"Gods, I've been waiting days to be able to do that."

I looked up to see Flynn looming over me, a maniacal grin splitting his face.

"Blue!" Lucian rushed to my side, trying to help me up but I was already getting to my feet.

"What the hell?!" I shook my head to clear my eyes. "You picked the wrong girl to mess with." Sparks and fire engulfed my hands ready to annihilate this boy. A line of fire enveloped the blade of my sword.

Lucian went to rush Flynn but I waved him away. I would take care of this problem.

"No, you did," he spat, but his voice had dramatically changed, from pubescent boy to something dark and dangerous… and feminine.

Then he started to change.

Flynn's body twisted grotesquely, like someone was pulling taffy, until it lengthened another two feet. Another set of arms sprouted from the ribcage, emitting a horrendous cracking sound, and a long serpentine tail grew from just above the butt. Groaning, he seemed to fold into himself—he looked like he was in pain—then he suddenly uncoiled, bursting upwards.

He was no longer Flynn. The small, eager boy with wide eyes and sunny disposition vanished. He was something altogether different—a terrifying amalgamation of snake, insect, and winged female demon with huge horns curling out of her head.

"It's an Empusa!" someone shouted from the shrieking crowd of people around me. I thought it was Achilles who had spoken, but I couldn't be sure.

"Aphrodite sends her regards," the creature hissed, then her tail whipped out at me.

The tip of it snapped at my face, and my skin split open from its razor sharp edge. It should've hurt, but I knew I had so much adrenaline coursing through my blood that I wouldn't feel it until it was all over. That would be the one and only shot it got.

I flung out my left hand, shooting lightning into her body, while I charged forward, swinging the sword. Twisting her form, she partially deflected the bolt with her big wing. The sparks burned a hole through the wing's membrane, but it wasn't the damage I'd hoped to cause. The blade of my sword thankfully sliced through one of her arms, leaving it dangling grotesquely by a ribbon of muscle.

The Empusa shrieked and reached for me. I was able to duck under one arm, but another snuck up right after it, grasped me by the throat, and yanked me forward. I dropped the sword.

"You're going to die!" she hissed in my face. Spittle landed on my cheeks, making my guts roil.

Panic started to rise, my heart pounding hard against my ribcage, as it opened its mouth and two sets of razor sharp teeth seemed about to sink into my head.

The demon suddenly reared back shrieking, blood spewing from its mouth. Her hand let go of my throat, and I buckled onto the ground. When I glanced up, I saw Lucian with Medusa's crimson coated sword in his hand. He'd stabbed the Empusa in the side. Jasmine and a few others stood in front of a still convulsing Cassandra, the new recruits had ran back to the academy. I spotted Medusa standing nearby, watching intently, although I didn't expect any help from her at all.

Normally, a wound like the one Lucian had inflicted would've been fatal, but the Empusa wasn't normal. She was a shapeshifting beast. Still bleeding profusely, she swung her tail around to strike me. I was able to dodge it but just barely—still winded from almost being strangled and mauled to death. I scrambled to the side, and rose to my feet with a fire ball forming in my hands. I flung it at the creature.

The fire hit her right in the chest, but it didn't burn. The flames seemed to flare around her body then snuff out instantly. She turned her head toward me and grinned, black lips coated in her blood. *Shit.* The demon was obviously fireproof.

For a second, I debated, trying to figure out how to kill her. I could drown her in a water cyclone I'd create from the water droplets in the air, or bury her deep in the earth by opening up a chasm in the ground. Yet, that made me think about Revana, and I hesitated for too long.

The Empusa launched at me, mouth open, teeth bared, and clawed hands reaching for my throat. Before it could reach me, a bright light flashed over us. The creature stopped in her tracks and shrunk against the glare. Squinting, I turned to see Cassandra hovering in the air, arms outstretched in the shape of a cross, her mouth open in a silent scream, and wide eyes engulfed in white. A blinding light beamed from them. Her hair floated around her head like she was floating in water.

"Protect her!" I heard someone shout from above, and I looked up to see Apollo swooping down from the sky. He landed in front of Cassandra, wings unfurled to their full span, acting like a shield. "She's a prophet! She mustn't be harmed!"

Everyone gaped at the scene, including the Empusa. I took the small window I had, ran for the sword laying on the ground, and flung it like a dagger at the beast. The large blade rang true, boring right through her heart.

With a scream, she clutched the hilt of the sword and I wasn't sure if it was going to try to pull it out, but even if she did, it was too late. The damage was done. More blood poured from her mouth as she collapsed to her knees, then toppled over onto her side. The Empusa's ragged breaths rattled in her throat until the drifted off, and she died. I stood over the dead body and felt sick to my stomach, especially when her face shifted back to that of the ginger-haired boy named Flynn.

When I looked up again to find the others, Cassandra floated over to where I stood. The light had gone from her eyes, but they were still white, rolled back in her head. She bent her head down to look at me.

"You are going to disappear into oblivion, Melany Richmond."

MELANY

*W*hat the hell?

Before I could react to that ominous declaration, Cassandra dropped from the sky, but I managed to catch her before she hit the ground. As I gently held her, her eyelids fluttered.

"No one will remember who you are," she spoke again. "You won't exist anymore." Then she slumped in my arms, her eyes closing.

Apollo raced over and took her from me, nearly pushing me over onto my ass. "Don't hurt her."

What? My eyebrows furrowed at his accusation. "I wasn't going to hurt her. She fell on me."

Apollo drew her hair away from her pale gaunt face. "I felt her power from across the academy. I've never known another prophet with this much intensity before."

"So, you're saying her predictions will come true?" I asked, a rush of shivers running down my back.

Apollo glanced over at me. "Yes."

"Awesome." I threw up my hands. "Just what I needed to hear right now."

Coming to my side, both Lucian and Jasmine helped me to my feet. "Mel, are you all right?" Jasmine asked.

"Well, apparently not. I'm going to disappear soon."

Lucian looked me over, probably searching for more injuries. He reached for my cheek, but I pulled away. "I'm okay. It'll heal. It'll just be one more scar to add to my collection."

"I need to get her to the infirmary." Apollo lifted Cassandra into his arms, unfolded his majestic white wings, and slowly rose into the air. He flew over the academy and onto the other side where the infirmary was located.

Lucian peered down at the Empusa. "I guess we know where your sense of danger was coming from."

Jasmine shook her head. "I can't believe what I just saw."

"Me either," I sighed.

She pulled me into a hug. It felt good to be embraced by my friend again. I'd feared I'd pushed her too far away for her to come back.

Achilles, Bellerophon, and Medusa surrounded the body. Medusa poked at it with the toe of her boot. "Ugly looking creatures, aren't they?"

"Effective though," Achilles admitted with a bit of admiration in his voice. Obviously, I knew who else not to trust.

"It wasn't that effective though. Now, was it?" I snapped. "I'm still alive."

He didn't comment, but he and Bellerophon reached down and picked up the body. Together, they carried it off the training field. After Medusa gathered her swords, wiping the blood on her pants, she gave me a little salute and followed them back to the school.

I rubbed at my neck. It was going to be sore for a while.

"Do you want to go see Chiron for some ointment for your throat, and to see if he can stitch up your cheek and shoulder?" Lucian asked.

"Yeah, I should." Without it, it would take days for them to heal, and I really didn't want to deal with the annoyance of it while I still had other things to do. Like finding Thanatos and finding out what was happening.

The three of us took to the sky to soar over the academy spires and to the other wing, where the infirmary was. I had to suppress the urge to just fly away and disappear.

Was that what this prophetess was talking about? My tendency to just up and go?

It wouldn't do any good right now; besides, it would also give me a chance to find out what I could about this Cassandra. Was she the "she" that Lucian's brother had told him about? Maybe she was our missing puzzle piece.

When we walked into the infirmary Apollo was there with Chiron, standing over Cassandra's unconscious form on one of the cots. She was so still that she looked dead. If I didn't spot the slight rise of her scrawny chest, I would've assumed she was.

Chiron looked up as we approached. "What are you three doing here?" When we got closer, he shook his head. "Oh. Yeah that looks like it needs stitches."

After showing him my shoulder, I also arched my neck to show him what I was sure were marks on my skin. When I swallowed, it still felt like her fingers were pressed into my flesh. "Hoping you have something to help with this, too."

He inspected my throat, then nodded. "Yeah, I have some cream you can apply." He moved toward the shelves and drawers where he kept all his medicinal supplies, pulling out a small glass jar. Inside it was a greenish cream and he handed it to me.

"Dab some of this on. It might feel tingly but that means it's working. It's got knitbone in it, and other powerful herbs."

I opened it and smoothed the sticky cream over my neck. He was right about the tingling sensation, it was instantaneous. I slid the jar into my pocket as Chiron took a needle and thread, stitching my cheek closed. Once he was done, he put on a bandage.

"That can come off in a day or two."

I then joined Apollo, Lucian, and Jasmine as they stood by the girl's cot.

"Will she wake up?" I asked.

Apollo nodded. "Yes. I just put her mind to sleep for a little bit."

"Is she dangerous?"

He gave me a withering look. "Of course not." Then he went back to gawking at Cassandra. The way he looked at her reminded me of someone who'd been awe-struck. It was how some girls regarded Lucian.

"She's extraordinary. I've never felt such power, especially not from someone so young." He reached down and grasped her hand. "There hasn't been a prophet born in a thousand years. It's not a coincidence that she's been called to the academy."

Lucian and I shared a look.

"Could she give you a vision?" I asked. "Like a dream?"

Apollo nodded, then his eyes narrowed at us. "Why are you asking?"

I thought about telling him, but I kept my lips shut. He wasn't necessarily what I'd call a friend, or even an ally. He'd been part of Zeus's plan to solidify power in the Gods' Army, and he'd tortured Lucian to find out information about me. Lucian swore that he didn't think Apollo had done it freely, that there had been some coercion on Zeus's part, but I wasn't so sure.

In my mind, those who weren't actively helping me, were against me.

Instead of answering, another thought crossed my mind. "Do prophets know everything that's going to happen? Or why it's happening?"

Apollo shook his head. "No. They can't actively pull out a prophecy from their minds. Portents come to them in powerful, sometimes painful, visions. It takes a toll on their minds."

I frowned. That was too bad. I was hoping she could tell me what was going on with Thanatos. Still, as

I looked her over, I realized she might prove useful. If Apollo was right and she'd been called to the academy for a reason, then helping me find Death, or the Fates, could be that reason.

Chiron frowned at us. "Don't you have other things to do right now? I really don't need the three of you hanging around while I'm working."

"No, not really," I admitted.

He gave me a look that said I shouldn't push him.

Jasmine grabbed my hand. "Let's go find Gina, Mia, and Ren, and get some ice cream. I think you two have some things to tell us."

She was right. Lucian and I did have a whole slew of things to tell our friends, and telling them over ice cream sounded perfect right about now. I also needed a long nap. It had been one hell of a day to be sure.

At least one thing had been solved: I found out the source of my ominous dread. I just couldn't believe that Aphrodite had sent someone to kill me. Although, really, the idea shouldn't have been that much of a surprise. She did threaten me when she was arrested and taken to Tartarus. She vowed to get her revenge.

Jasmine had also been right about the ice cream. It had been perfect, and seeing my friends and confiding in them about everything that had happened felt cathartic. Way more than the "counselling" sessions with Psyche, which Prometheus had set up for us.

Technically, we were all a bunch of wounded soldiers, each with an injury whether physical, mental, or spiritual that we were trying to deal with, but I usually clutched onto my pain, secreting it away. I didn't want to constantly talk about it like the others did. I figured a lot of the boys used the sessions as a way to just stare at Psyche—she was incredibly pretty with big boobs.

Not too long ago, Jasmine told me that she thought I didn't want to get through my problems. That I wanted to wallow in my misery and pain. I'd been offended when she first said it, but she was probably right. I liked a good pain wallow. Kept me honest.

Yet, sitting with my friends in the dining hall, gorging on mountains of ice cream and sprinkles while telling them about my dreams, and my conversations with Persephone and Hephaistos felt amazing. It felt like confession, and in a way, I supposed I was looking to be absolved of my sins... as they were plenty.

When I made my way through the academy halls to my room, in the dark, I was actually feeling pretty good. Until I was accosted by a shadowy form and dragged into a dark alcove.

Tisiphone's blood red eyes trained on me. "Come with me," she demanded.

"Gods, you scared me. What do you want?"

"I know where Thanatos is. Do you want to meet with him or not?"

My breathing halted with her confession. "Yeah, of course I do."

"Then, quit whining and come with me." She stepped back into the corridor, visibly shuddering. "Ugh, I hate this place. I don't know how you can stand it."

"It's not that bad."

She grunted.

We quickly walked down the hall together to an exit. Her gaze kept sweeping back and forth as we moved.

"Hey, where's that golden boy of yours? Is he around here somewhere? I'd love to take a big juicy bite out of him. He looks like a deliciously sweet, yellow pear."

"You're not going to eat Lucian."

"You're no fun up here."

Before we reached the doors, I considered for a moment going to see Lucian to tell him where I was going. I'd taken off so many times without telling him that I felt like maybe I owed it to him to do it now. Yet,

I could see how impatient Tisiphone was acting, and I feared she wouldn't wait for me. I was sure I'd be back before morning.

Once outside, Tisiphone opened her wings and immediately flew up into the air. My wings unfolded from my back, and I joined her in the sky. Before I got too high, I glanced down and spotted Demeter near the maze, looking upward. She shook her head at me, but it was too late to do anything about that.

The Fury and I flew over the academy and toward the lake. I wondered if we were going down to the underworld through the tree stump, although I was sure Tisiphone could travel the shadows without problems. If I was with her, I'd be able to as well, but she didn't swoop down to the lake. She led us over it, and started to descend on the other side, toward a large wooded area. An area none of us had really investigated before tonight.

Once on the ground, she walked into the trees, then stopped at a wide green plant that had large white flowers blooming from it. The flowers looked like pinwheels.

She caught me looking at the plant. "It's called daruga, or the Devil's Trumpet. The flowers usually only bloom at night."

I frowned. "Is this some kind of doorway? Like under the plant or something?"

"Nope." She unsheathed the large bejeweled dagger at her waist. "But this is." She raised the knife in the air, and drew it down all the way to the ground.

At first I thought she was crazy, but when I squinted and turned my head to the right just slightly, I noticed a flap, like curled paper, in the air in front of her.

After putting her blade away, she took hold of the flap, and pulled to reveal a dark entrance way in the very air where no entrance could possibly exist. Tisiphone's leg disappeared the moment she stepped into it, and she looked at back at me. "Are you coming, or what?"

A few seconds later, she seemed to vanish into thin air, but had really torn open this existence and walked into another. Swallowing down the anxiety, I grabbed the flap like Tisiphone had done, pulled it open. Inside, all I could see was darkness. I counted to three under my breath, then stepped through the hole.

Once I was through, I briefly looked over my shoulder to see a narrow slice of daylight, and the grass and trees. It was insane. I blinked several times to adjust to the gloom around me. Eventually, I could see that we were standing in a dark field that seemed to go on forever, at the base of a soaring circular staircase that looked constructed from stars. It wound up into the sky and vanished into the shadows above us.

"Holy shit," I muttered under my breath. Obviously, Tisiphone heard me because she grinned.

"It's pretty amazing isn't it?"

"What is it? And where does it go?"

"It's a staircase, stupid." She shook her head. "It goes to Nyx's temple in the sky."

"Is that where Thanatos is?"

She shrugged. "That's what I heard. He literally went home to Mommy."

MELANY

"The Goddess of Night is Thanatos mother?" I made a face.

"Yes, duh. Where did you think he came from?"

I guess I never really thought about it. Death was death. I never considered he would have been born. I assumed that he just existed. It was really strange to think he had a mother.

Tisiphone started up the stairs, and I followed her close behind without hesitation. Each step was made up of several white glowing stars touching points, but because there was pitch darkness between them, I found it disorienting. When I stepped forward, in some instances, it looked like I was stepping onto nothing.

A few times I lost my balance, and flailed my arms to find something to grab. For the most part, I found a hand railing made of the night, but once I ended up grabbing onto Tisiphone's leg. I may have inadvertently touched her butt. She kicked back at me once, and I nearly toppled off the edge of the staircase.

I didn't know how far we'd climbed, but when I looked down over the side, I could barely see the field below us. Mind you, it was nightfall all around us, so there wasn't much to see anyway. When we finally reached the top, I was breathless. It was either from climbing so many stairs, or the fact that the air felt thin up here.

Looming before us was an imposing, grandiose temple, built from smooth black marble. Moonlight bathed the building, like a spotlight, and I could see each column had carvings in them. My breath caught in my throat looking at it. I'd seen castles of white stone, and halls of gold, but neither compared to the stunning majesty of the Temple of Night.

Tisiphone climbed the three steps to the entrance. My legs felt like rubber, but I followed. A sense of dread washed over me.

The Fury eyed me. "You're not scared, are you?"

"No," I sputtered, although I might have been lying. The lump in my throat told another story as we walked through the columns and into the building.

Moonlight streamed through large window openings on each side, easily showing the way. Although, there wasn't much to see at that point. The lofty hall was empty. There were no sofas to lounge on, no chairs to sit, no tables to set anything on, it was just stark and cold.

Our footsteps echoed against the dark marble floor, dome ceiling, and walls with each movement, but other sounds filtered beyond that. Shuffling, and scratching noises, reminding me a bit of when Arachne had scuttled out of the large crack in the foundry roof. Out of the corners of my eyes, I saw swift movement in the darkest corners of the building, along the floor, and on the ceiling. Something—actually, a bunch of some-things—were following us.

Tisiphone led us across what I realized was an inner chamber, then we came to a large set of stone doors. She pushed them open, entering another large room. I followed close behind, completely aware that something as small as a cat rode my heels. Honestly, I was afraid to turn around and see what it was.

The next chamber was larger than the last, but just as barren. Moonlight filtered in through several narrow slits, stretching along the expanse of each wall. A few long steps leading to a dais sat at the end of the room, with a throne made of dark stone carved to look like a huge raven. Inside those arced black wings sat a form. I couldn't completely make it out, whether it was male or female, or neither, but there was no mistaking the glowing white orbs staring at us as we approached.

When Tisiphone reached the bottom of the dais, she dropped to one knee and bowed her head. Unsure of exactly what was going on and who she was bowing to, I mimicked her, just in case. As I slowly raised my head, I saw who sat on the throne.

The woman looked like she was made of night itself, with jet black skin and long, luxurious black hair. Except, it was hard to distinguish what was her flesh, and what was her dress—though I was sure she was wearing one. Her eyes were illuminated stars set into her face, and when she blinked, it seemed like strobe lights. A crescent moon shape glowed on her forehead. At first, I thought it was some sort of jewel as part of a headpiece, or crown, but then realized it was just part of her.

This was Nyx, Goddess of the Night, and mother to Death.

"Thank you for allowing us to enter your realm," Tisiphone offered.

Nyx raised a hand, motioning for us to stand. We did, but I felt very fidgety, nervously shifting my weight from foot to foot. Tisiphone glared at me, but it wasn't enough to make me stop.

When she opened her mouth, the words seemed to stream out on a thread of a whisper that circled us. "What do you want?"

It made me shiver, like being caressed by a cool breeze.

Tisiphone went to answer, but I beat her to it. This was my quest. "I need to talk to Thanatos."

The Fury gave me a scathing look, but I ignored it. I was used to her disdain.

Nyx's eyes focused on me. It was like staring down headlights from an oncoming semi-truck. "Who are you to demand such a thing?"

"I'm Melany. Thanatos knows me."

"If Death truly knew you, you wouldn't be standing here," she challenged.

I shrugged. "What can I tell you? We've met a few times, had a conversation, and I'm still here."

I didn't think she liked my attitude; a gust of cold wind blew through the room in response, nearly knocking me backward.

"You can go now. Either by the stairs, or I can toss you over the edge."

What was it with Goddesses wanting to throw me off the edge of things? Persephone had done it twice, and Tisiphone had nearly done it on the way up here.

"I don't think you understand." I moved forward, placing my foot on one of the steps. "I need to talk with him, and I'm not leaving until I do."

"You truly are an idiot, aren't you?" Tisiphone murmured between clenched teeth.

Nyx rose to her feet, her hair and her dress billowed out around her like black seaweed floating on the ocean's surface. I could feel her presence pressing down on me, and I had to fight the urge to drop to my knees in front of her.

"It is you who does not understand." She lifted her hand. "With a snap of my fingers I could render you extinct. You wouldn't die, and go to Elysium. You would be nowhere, be nothing. It would be like you never existed. No one would remember your name."

Dread poured into me, and I swallowed. *Well, damn girl, that's quite the effective threat.*

The air shimmered on the dais near the throne, then from seemingly nowhere, Erebus, the God of the Shadows and my former professor, stepped out of the darkness. He still looked like a Victorian era vampire, garbed in tails, a top hat, and carrying a black and silver cane.

"Allow her to talk with Thanatos," he intervened.

Nyx cut him with a harsh glance. "And why should I do that?"

When he set his hand on her arm, she seemed to melt against it. Interesting. Who knew that Erebus had game? "I know Melany, she has an affinity to the shadows and to darkness. She could be useful to you."

Nyx's gaze focused on me again, and it was hard to hold her gaze, but I did. "I highly doubt that." She waved her hand toward us. "Leave my realm. Now."

Surprised, I reared back. "But I must speak with him. It's a matter of life and death… and fate."

Her eyes glowed even brighter, and I had to avert my gaze or risk burning my retinas. "What do I care of the life and death of mortals?"

"Technically, I'm a demigod…" That obviously didn't make any difference to her, because the room grew even colder. An icy breeze blasted against my skin, and I started to shiver.

"Leave my sight now, this is your last warning."

Tisiphone grabbed my arm and pulled me away. "Let's go."

I let her guide me out of the room, but I had no intention of leaving.

Once we were outside the temple, I unfurled my

wings and flapped them a few times to test the air density, seeing how easily it would be to fly up here.

"What are you doing?" Tisiphone spat incredulously.

"I'm going to find Death and have a conversation. I didn't come all this way for nothing." After a couple more flaps I lifted from the ground. The air was a lot thinner up here, so it didn't take much energy to fly. "Are you coming with me?"

"Hell no. You're on your own." She marched toward the staircase without a single look over her shoulder.

I let her go. I didn't need her anyway. She got me here, that was all that mattered.

I flew up to hover over the temple. There had to be another way in, another chamber or room where Thanatos was hiding. I decided to circle the building to get a better idea about its construction. As I swooped around, I saw that there was a large open area in the back that seemed very much like a garden. It had lofty trees and blooming flowers, a pond with a fountain spouting water, and even a few stone benches peppered around it. On one of those benches I spotted a cloaked figure smoking weed—by the pungent stink that wafted up to my nose—and near his feet was another cloaked figure face down on the ground.

I quickly dove toward the garden and landed smoothly next to the bench. The cloaked figure on the bench looked up at me, at least I think he did, as there was no face inside the hood just empty darkness.

"Thanatos? I need to speak to you."

The cloaked figure on the bench, took a drag of the joint, then nudged the other on the ground with his foot. "Dude, there's someone here to see you."

Flipping over, he focused empty eyes on me. "Melany?" his voice was as raspy as ever.

"Thanatos?" I glanced at the figure on the bench. "Then who are you?"

"I'm Hypnos, his brother." He nudged Thanatos again with his foot. "Get up, you fool." And glanced back at me, "He's depressed. Been here like that for a couple of days."

I stared down at Death again, completely flabbergasted at what I was hearing. How could Death be depressed? Made no sense.

Hypnos stretched out his arms, then sighed. "Well, time for me to go. I got a bunch of people I've got to put to sleep." He stood, then handed me the blunt. "Want the rest?"

"No, thanks."

He pinched off the end, then put the joint inside a pocket in his cloak.

As he started to walk out of the garden, I heard a thunderous sound, followed by an orchestra of peeps and shrieks. From the top of the temple, an undulating cloud of darkness swarmed toward us. The closer it got, the more it seemed like a flock of deformed bats. When it was right upon us, I realized they weren't bats, but some kind of demonic creature with black leathery skin and glowing red eyes. One landed on top of Hypnos' head and hissed down at me.

"Come, my pets, we have dreams to spawn." He left the garden, his demon pets flocking around him, until he seemed to walk right of the edge of the sky and disappeared.

When he was gone, Thanatos got onto his knees, crawled to the bench pulling himself onto it with a long breathy sigh. "What are you doing here?"

I sat beside him. "I came to see you. I need to ask you about the Fates, and what is going on with them."

He shrugged. "I wish I knew. I haven't heard from them in days."

"Is that why you are depressed?"

"Yes," he whined. "I haven't been able to take anyone's soul. No one is dying. What's the point of my existence, if I can't ferry souls to their eternities?"

"What do you mean no one is dying?"

"It means just that. No mortals, demigods, or Gods

are dying. Remember that man who had a heart attack on the dock?"

"Yeah?"

"Well, he died. I should've been able to take his soul and take him where he needed to go, but he didn't quite die."

"I saved him…"

He shook his head. "No, you didn't. It was his time to die. His thread was shown to me days before, but when I came to get him, his soul wouldn't leave his body."

"So, there have been no deaths anywhere in the world? Not even if someone is shot in the head, they won't die?"

"They could have their heart ripped out and they won't be dead. They'd just be walking around with literally no heart inside their body."

I cringed at the thought. "Have you gone to talk to the Fates? Surely, they have their reasons for—,

"No one talks to the Fates. There is no "going to talk to them". That doesn't happen."

"Why not?"

"Because no one knows where they live."

"In the Cave of Memory."

His blank head turned toward me, and I imagined if he had a face he'd be giving me some kind of stink eye. "I know it's the Cave of Memory, but I've been to every realm, above and below, and haven't found it. No one has."

Frowning, I sensed that wasn't true. In the vision Cassandra showed me, someone was there, so someone had to know. "Are you sure that absolutely no one has ever found their cave?"

Sighing, he slumped down on the bench, resting his head against the back. "There's an old story, but I don't know how true it is."

"Just tell me."

"Do you know the story about the Trojan War?"

I made a face. "A little. We learned about it in school. Basically it all started when Hera, Athena, and Aphrodite fought about who was the prettiest, and some guy named Paris chose Aphrodite. And then Aphrodite told Paris he couldn't have Helen of Troy as a wife, so he kidnapped her, then there was a big war over it. Oh, and Achilles fought with Troy against them all. I don't know. Sounds stupid and pointless, considering they are all friends now."

Death snorted. "There are no friends amongst the Gods. You should know that by now."

"Anyway…"

"Right, so what was not in the story books, was that Paris was mortally injured on the battlefield…"

"Wasn't he saved by some nymph named Oenone?"

"No, it wasn't Oenone who tried to save him. It was Aphrodite. It's said she was in love with him, so she found the Fates and begged them to save his life. They refused, and Paris died."

I knew Aphrodite had something to do with this! "So she knows where the Cave of Memory is."

He shrugged again. "It's a story, that's all I know."

Grabbing his hand, I shook it. "Thank you, Thanatos." I got to my feet, buoyed by his information. It at least gave me a path to follow. "And don't worry, I'm going to fix this and you'll be back to collecting souls once again."

Now, I just needed to figure out how to get into Tartarus so I could talk to Aphrodite.

A sudden icy wind blasted against my back, and I whipped around to find Nyx floating behind me. Her starry eyes flashed like tiny explosions.

"You! How dare you defy me?!"

I put my hands up in defence. "I'm sorry, but you really gave me no choice."

"There is always a choice," she rasped, "And you made yours."

She snapped her fingers.

Thank you for reading Demigods Academy 4. Don't miss **BOOK 5!**

We hope you enjoyed Melany's adventures and can't wait to share more with you. In the meantime, we would love to read your opinion on Amazon and Goodreads. Please consider leaving a review for us. **We'd love it.**

And if you don't want to miss our future books, you just need to join our lists of readers below.

Sign Up to get our EMAILS at:

www.KieraLegend.com

www.ElisaSAmore.com/Vip-List

Sign Up to get our SMS (US only):

Text AMORE to 77948

Text LEGEND to 77948

ABOUT THE AUTHOR

Kiera Legend writes Urban Fantasy and Paranormal Romance stories that bite. She loves books, movies and Tv-Shows. Her best friends are usually vampires, witches, werewolves and angels. She never hangs out without her little dragon. She especially likes writing kick-ass heroines and strong worldbuildings and is excited for all the books that are coming!

Text LEGEND to 77948 to don't miss any of them (US only) or sign up at www.kieralegend.com to get an email alert when her next book is out.

FOLLOW KIERA LEGEND:
facebook.com/groups/kieralegend
facebook.com/kieralegend
authorkieralegend@gmail.com

***

Elisa S. Amore is the number-one bestselling author of the paranormal romance saga *Touched*.

Vanity Fair Italy called her "the undisputed queen of romantic fantasy." After the success of Touched, she produced the audio version of the saga featuring Hollywood star Matt Lanter (*90210, Timeless, Star Wars*) and Disney actress Emma Galvin, narrator of *Twilight* and *Divergent*. Elisa is now a full-time writer of young adult fantasy. She's wild about pizza and also loves traveling, which she calls a source of constant inspiration. With her successful series about life and death, Heaven and Hell, she has built a loyal fanbase on social media that continues to grow, and has quickly become a favorite author for thousands of readers in the U.S.

Visit Elisa S. Amore's website and join her List of Readers at www.ElisaSAmore.com

Find Elisa S. Amore on: